PRAISE FOR THE HOWARD WALLACE P.I. SERIES

★". . . . an absolute delight, told with clear affection for the usual P.I. story tropes and injecting them with just the right amount of amusement while avoiding sarcastic mockery." —*BULLETIN OF THE CENTER FOR CHILDREN'S BOOKS* (STARRED REVIEW)

"Strong writing, relatable themes, and a solid mystery combine for a read that both boys and girls will have trouble putting down." —SCHOOL LIBRARY JOURNAL

"Give this to fans of Encyclopedia Brown who are looking for longer (and funnier!) well-plotted mysteries." —BOOKLIST

"Lyall's debut is a winner." —PUBLISHERS WEEKLY

"Mystery fans should enjoy it . . . [it lands] in new territory, and the characters interact realistically and have real kid problems. —KIRKUS REVIEWS

HOWARD WALLACE, P.I.

SABOTAGE STAGE LEFT

HOWARD WALLACE, P.I.

SABOTAGE STAGE LEFT

by Casey Lyall

STERLING CHILDREN'S BOOKS
New York

STERLING CHILDREN'S BOOKS
New York

An Imprint of Sterling Publishing Co., Inc.
1166 Avenue of the Americas
New York, NY 10036

ISBN 978-1-4549-2968-0

Distributed in Canada by Sterling Publishing Co., Inc.
c/o Canadian Manda Group, 664 Annette Street
Toronto, Ontario M6S 2C8, Canada
Distributed in the United Kingdom by GMC Distribution Services
Castle Place, 166 High Street, Lewes, East Sussex BN7 1XU, England
Distributed in Australia by NewSouth Books
45 Beach Street, Coogee, NSW 2034, Australia

For information about custom editions, special sales, and premium and
corporate purchases, please contact Sterling Special Sales at 800-805-5489
or specialsales@sterlingpublishing.com.

Manufactured in Canada

Lot #:
2   4   6   8   10   9   7   5   3   1
07/18

sterlingpublishing.com

Wallace and Mason Investigations

~~Mason and Wallace Investigations~~

Rules of Private Investigation
THE GOLDEN RULE: WE HELP PEOPLE.

1. Work with what you've got. *Especially when it's a fabulous shade of green.*

2. Ask the right questions.

3. Know your surroundings.

4. Always have a cover story ready.

5. Blend in.

6. A bad plan is better than no plan. *I think we need to revisit this rule. -No.*

7. Never underestimate your opponent.

8. Never tip your hand.

9. Don't get caught. *You should try following this rule, Howard.* *Stop it.*

10. Pick your battles.

11. Don't leave a trail.

12. Everyone has a hook.

13. *Always listen to your partner. She's a genius.* *Speaking of rules we need to revisit.* *Very funny.*

14. No more sports cases. (AGREED.)

Chapter One

"**S**ure that's the guy?"

The voice stretched across the hall over the hustle and bustle of lunchtime traffic. I bit back a laugh at the incredulous tone, steadying myself against the flow of bodies bumping by. End of the week, everyone got a bit clumsier, a little more careless. As I grabbed my bag out of my locker, I heard the scoffing reply:

"You see anybody else walking around in a bathrobe?"

Lucky coat. I tugged down a brown terrycloth sleeve. Big difference.

My partner bopped up to stand beside me. "Is that our twelve o'clock I see lurking over there?" Ivy rolled up on her tiptoes to peer over my shoulder. "They look twitchy."

"Waiting's good," I said. "Builds character."

"What?" Ivy slid me a sideways look. "Are we billing by the hour now?"

I snorted when she towed me down the hall, stepping up to the two waiting girls. They leapt to attention, one with an eager smile and the other keeping a wary eye.

"Caitlyn." Nodding at our client, I turned my attention to her watchful tagalong. "Didn't realize we'd have company. Who's your friend?"

The tiny, blond sixth grader flicked an impatient wave back at me. "This is Denice. She heard you were helping me and invited herself along." She rolled her eyes. "She said I shouldn't be meeting you by myself."

I could respect a healthy level of suspicion. "Nothing wrong with a little backup," I said. "Shall we take this into my office?" Holding open the door, I waited as Ivy and Caitlyn stepped inside. Denice leaned past me to look in, hovering at the threshold. "Well?" I waved her on.

"This is the girls' bathroom," she said, wrinkling her nose.

"I spend my time solving cases, not scoping out real estate. Be happy it's not the boys'." I walked into the room, letting the door swing shut behind me. It opened a crack as Denice scooted in and hurried over to Caitlyn's side.

"Why did you hire this guy?" She muttered down to Caitlyn, worrying the end of her braid with her fingers. "He's cranky."

"Because he gets results," I said, reaching into my pocket. I pulled out a USB stick and held it out to our client.

Caitlyn let out a shriek as she grabbed the stick from my hand. "You found it? Oh, my gosh. Thank you." She clutched it to her chest, eyes watering. "I was so worried. I thought it was lost forever. How did you find it?"

"Good old-fashioned legwork." Ivy boosted herself up on one of the sinks. "Got the schedule for the computer lab, made some inquiries, twisted a few arms. The usual." She swung her feet back and forth, hands braced behind her on the sides of the sink. "What's on that thing that's so important, anyway?"

I shot a look at my partner. Knowing our client's business was a world away from asking our client's business. Ivy shrugged, casually ignoring the confines of professional nosiness.

"Oh." Caitlyn blushed faintly. "It's my novel," she said. "I've been working on it since last year."

"Quite the treasure to leave lying around," I said. People let the small size of Grantleyville lull them into a false sense

3

of security. Their vulnerability made for our gain, but cases like Caitlyn's didn't always have a happy ending. "Should look at expanding your backup into digital."

Denice nodded sagely, a faint note of approval flashing behind her black-framed glasses. She pushed them up the bridge of her nose with a spindly finger. "That's what I keep telling her."

"I've got backup out the wazoo," Caitlyn said, dismissing our concerns with a shake of her head. "This is one of a billion copies. I was just worried about it getting lost and falling into the wrong hands. It's not ready for the world to read yet." She kissed the USB before stuffing it deep into her bag and stepped back to give me a beaming smile. "Ally was right about you."

Ivy perked up in her seat. "How so?"

"She said you were the ones who could help me," she said. "That you know your stuff. And she was so right!" Caitlyn threw herself forward, grabbing me in a viselike grip. "Thank you so, so much!"

I blinked at my partner who shook with silent laughter while I endured the crushing hug. "We aim to please," I said. "Now there is the small matter of your bill."

"Oh, yeah!" Caitlyn released her octopus hold and dug

through her pockets. "Here you go," she said, thrusting a crumpled envelope into my hands.

"How much did they charge you?" Denice asked under her breath.

"Not enough," Caitlyn said. "Seriously, I would have paid way more to get it back. You guys are worth every penny. Do you have more of those sticky notes? I want to give them to my friends."

"Business cards," I corrected, dragging a stack out from the depths of my coat. I pulled a few off the top and handed them over. "Glad we could be of service."

Denice dragged her friend out the door as Caitlyn continued to call out her thanks. Huffing out a breath, I set about straightening my hug-rumpled attire.

"Another happy customer," Ivy said cheerfully. "And it sounds like we should think about upping our rates." She tapped a finger against her lips. "Who's Ally?"

I racked my brain. "No clue."

"Word must be getting around." Ivy rubbed her hands together, cackling.

A toilet flushed, and we both froze. I whipped around to glare at my partner.

"You didn't check the stalls," I said.

"You were supposed to check them," Ivy shot back.

"I was talking to our client," I said, one eye on the stall door swinging open. A tall girl emerged, hitching her bag over one shoulder. She walked up to the sink, studiously ignoring us, and began washing her hands.

"Hi." Ivy said, leaning over from her perch on the neighboring sink. "Wallace and Mason Investigations. How's it going?"

The girl shook out her hands and scooted around Ivy to the paper towel dispenser. We stood in silence, listening to the roll crunch forward as she pulled out three pieces in quick succession.

"I swear we're very organized and efficient," Ivy continued. "Here for all of your investigative needs."

That earned Ivy an eyebrow-raise as the girl chucked her paper towels in the garbage. It sailed in with a light swish, and I handed her one of our cards before she headed out the door.

"Tell your friends," Ivy said to her retreating back.

"Smooth." I dragged a hand over my face as the door closed. "Stall checks, Ivy," I said.

"That was super smooth!" Ivy hopped off the sink to waggle a finger at me. "And yes, I missed the stall checks, but maybe we got a new client out of it? More importantly, we still haven't figured out who Ally is."

"Word must be getting around," I said. "People have heard about the agency and the cases we've solved."

"What I'm hearing is that we have fans." Ivy did a little dance stopping abruptly midmove to stare at me.

I took a step back. "What?"

She leaned in, narrowing her gaze into a squint. "There's something wrong with your face. Your cheeks are all squished up." She pinched at her own. "And I can see your teeth? It's weird. I think we should go see the nurse."

"Shut up." I ran a hand over my mouth, but it was no help against the smile stretching it from side to side. "I'm not used to attention without violence attached to it. Or detention. Let me enjoy the moment."

"Yes," Ivy said, diving into her bag to rummage around for her lunch. "Enjoy it, my friend." She raised her water bottle. "Cheers to Ally. May she continue to provide us with free advertising—whoever she is."

I tipped my drink against hers, and we settled down onto the floor to eat our lunch. Stuffing my returning grin full of sandwich, I fully enjoyed the moment. I'd been at the detective thing for close to a year now. Ivy'd been on board since the fall, and we'd slowly but surely put a team together. We'd worked a few major cases so I wasn't completely surprised how far news had spread, but I couldn't deny it was nice to have people uttering my name with a positive ring for a change. Felt like a step in the right direction.

If only that step wasn't trailing toilet paper.

"I miss having a proper office," I said, glancing around at the paint peeling off the walls and the water-spotted ceiling.

Ivy's head snapped up at that. "You miss having a broken-down desk held up by pickle buckets? Outside in the open elements? Left vulnerable to squirrel attacks?"

"When you put it like that," I said. "Yes. Yes, I do." I flapped a hand at the dripping sinks and gurgling toilets. "It's not like we're currently putting our best foot forward. I miss having our own space. We need better digs."

"Hard to find better digs when we're not supposed to be investigating on school property in the first place," Ivy said. "It's called keeping a low profile."

Being banned from conducting any at-school investigations put a major cramp in our activities. That rule was laid down months ago. Now that they'd had some time to cool off, I felt fairly certain that the administration would agree with my 'what they don't see won't enrage them' policy. Hence the bathroom base of operations.

"Like anyone's paying attention to what we're doing these days," I said. "It's spring musical city out there, and we're sliding right under the radar."

Ivy made a noise of agreement as she chewed her cookie.

"You still doing okay with all of that?" I asked. "Doing this stuff and the musical? We'll survive if you need to take more of a break."

Ivy joined the Grantleyville Middle School Drama Club as part of a cover story for an investigation a few months back. The case was long closed, but she'd enjoyed the group enough to stick around. Why was a mystery I had yet to solve. The club was putting on *Little Shop of Horrors* for the spring musical and Ivy was helping both on stage and off. With only two weeks left to showtime, it was all hands on deck.

"This was probably my last job for the next couple weeks," Ivy admitted. "We're going to have more rehearsals leading up to opening night and Mrs. Pamuk doesn't want anyone missing one if we can help it."

"Makes sense," I said. "I pushed our meeting back so I can still help out after school."

Ivy choked a bit on her cookie, and I patted her on the back. "That's okay," she croaked out, brushing a chunk of curly brown hair out of her face. "You don't have to come by. I know you're busy."

"I'm not going to leave my partner in the lurch." I grinned at Ivy. "I can spare an hour to do some grunt work."

"Yeah," Ivy said. "Yes, for sure. You should definitely come help. That would be great."

That was about three confirmations too many. Ivy was cast in the musical back in February, and I'd recently started to help out as the behind-the-scenes action picked up. I thought things had been running smoothly up until now. "Or not," I said. "I can hang around until you're done." Never let it be said Howard Wallace can't take a hint.

"No," Ivy said. "I want you there. It's—some of the crew members were underappreciative of your handiwork from last time."

"Everything went great!"

"Howard, you nailed your pants to the backdrop," she said, ignoring my attempts to wave her off. "While you were wearing them."

"That's fine," I said with a shrug. "I don't have to work on the construction side. I can paint."

Ivy caught her flinch before her shoulders followed through.

"What." Toddlers can paint. What possible complaint could there be about my painting skills?

"I just—" She let out a little high-pitched hum. "I mean, you remember what the home office looks like, right?"

Built by Pops and myself. Not a masterpiece by most standards, but serviceable. In the right wind conditions.

"That was artistic license," I said. "Those gaps are for aesthetic purposes only. It only dried like that because they mixed it wrong. I can paint. I'll follow the instructions. It'll be *fine*."

Chapter Two

I could not paint.

It should be straightforward. Put paint on brush. Put brush on canvas.

But the brush and the paint were in a conspiracy against me with gravity as the mastermind. A swath of red-streaked canvas mocked my efforts.

"Should the paint be chunky?" Ivy popped up behind me, resting her chin on my shoulder. "Or is that another artistic choice?"

"Very funny," I said, tossing the brush back into the paint tray. We stood back to look at the backdrop together and I sighed. So much for being helpful.

"No, no, I like it! Looks good," she said. "It's like a 3D effect. It makes the flowers really pop."

I slid a sideways look at my partner. "It's supposed to be bricks."

Ivy blinked at the stretched-out canvas, tilting her head to the side. She kept leaning until she was bent over at the waist. "Oh, yeah," she said. "I see it now."

"You're the worst."

"Nice job on the flowers, Howard." I looked over my shoulder at the source of the voice as Ivy dissolved into giggles on the floor. Miles Fletcher towered behind me, attempting to look encouraging while ignoring the laughing mess on the floor.

"It's supposed to be the outside of the flower shop, not the inside," I said with a sigh.

"Ooooh." Miles winced. "Well, maybe I can give you a hand." He picked up a paint stick and started scraping off some of the more visible lumps from the backdrop.

If you'd asked me at the beginning of the year whether or not I could see myself working on the same side as Miles for any cause, I'd have laughed in your face. For a good long time. But after an intense dognapping case back in February, we talked through some of our issues. Now my former best friend was a current Temporary Junior Freelance Associate of Wallace and Mason Investigations. It was a bit much to fit on a business card, but the sliver of glee I felt every time he complained was enough to keep me from changing it. Just because we were semifriendly didn't mean I couldn't have my fun.

My partner picked herself up off the floor and grabbed the paint brush. "I think with a little more definition and a few extra coats," she said. "We can make this work."

"Sounds like a plan." I turned up my sleeves.

Ivy pointed her brush at me. "Miles and I can take care of this, Howard. Why don't you take a breather?"

"You sure?"

"Positive," Ivy said. "We've got it covered. Take a spin around. There's a ton of stuff to do and not nearly enough people. I guarantee someone could use the help."

Effectively ejected from my post, I scanned the gym, looking for another area where I could pitch in. The theater world wasn't my scene, but it was important to Ivy, and I was determined to learn the ins and outs. Kids filled up every corner of the room—working on costumes, running lines, patching up props. It was a hive of activity where everyone had a task. There had to be *something* I could contribute to.

A table across the room caught my eye. Scotty Harris was stationed there, layering strips of green fabric over a chicken wire frame. He was a member of the band and the basketball team, a casual associate of our agency, and apparently now part of the Drama Club. I could work with Scotty.

I strode over to his table, ready to roll up my sleeves and dive in. "Scotty," I said, reaching up to clap him on the shoulder.

He jumped in the air and flipped around to face me, eyes wide. "Oh, Howard," he said, darting a glance between me and the table. "Startled me. I didn't hear you come up. Probably because you're a detective and you're good at being sneaky."

At least one of us was. It was hard to miss the way he was inching his way to stand between me and his project.

"We should put a bell on you, heh, heh," Scotty said. "I guess that wouldn't be great though with you being a detective, right? Maybe if you were a cat detective. But then—"

"Ivy and Miles took over my painting project," I said, cutting off any further thoughts on cat detectives. "Came over here to see if I could lend a hand."

"Got two working pretty well together already." Scotty brandished his hands at me. "Probably shouldn't split them up. They're used to each other by now." He chuckled nervously again. "But thanks! Thanks for the offer."

"What is this thing anyway?" I ducked around him to get a closer look at the table.

Scotty's jaw dropped. "This is Audrey II."

"That explained nothing."

"She's only the star of the show, Howard," Scotty said, patting the wiry frame. "The plant from outer space? Seymour's pet that starts it all? She puts the 'horror' in *Little Shop of Horrors*?"

"*What* is this play about?" I shook my head, trying to put the pieces into place.

Scotty frowned. "Ivy hasn't explained it to you yet?"

"Oh, she's tried," I said. "But every time I ask and she starts in, it always ends in her singing all the songs and trying to teach me the moves."

"Ashi's the same way," Scotty said. "I've been helping her practice and—"

Mrs. Pamuk, the teacher advisor for the Drama Club, began clapping her hands, putting a pin in Scotty's attempt to educate me. "All right, kids," she said. "That's all the time we have for today. Those of you attending rehearsal this week-end, I will not be there, but Mrs. Grantley-Smythe will see you bright and early tomorrow at the senior center. Everyone else, see you Monday. Let's get this place cleaned up before we go. Parker?" She gestured at a weedy boy standing beside her, and he immediately leapt into action.

I rolled my eyes at Scotty as Parker Bowman spat out rapid-fire instructions to the rest of the group. A ninth grader from Grantleyville High, Parker showed up a few weeks ago and slithered his way into the prime spot of Student Director.

"You okay here?" I checked in with Scotty before heading back to Miles and Ivy. Their mess was going to require significantly more cleanup than his. He nodded, shooing me away from his table, and I wound my way back through the crowd.

"I want to see costumes hung up neatly," Parker hollered. "Those props need to be properly labeled and stored. There's no excuse for sloppy behavior. That's why things go missing, and we don't have any more time for that. You might be in middle school, but you can still be professional."

Like Parker would know anything about being a professional. It only took one rehearsal, one afternoon of his lectures, of listening to him chew out a crew member, for me to take his measure and find him lacking. I wasn't alone in that assessment.

"I can't stand that guy," Miles said. "Who comes back here after you've made it to high school? How does he not have better things to do?"

"Mrs. Pamuk said he was getting volunteer credits for helping out or something?" Ivy shrugged.

"Does he get extra credits on a sliding scale of bossiness?" I asked as I walked up and began stacking the paint cans. We managed to get the spills cleaned up and most of the equipment put away before catching Parker's eye. Ivy and Miles were folding up the drop cloths as I collected the rest of the gear when he strode over.

"Mason, Wallace, Fletcher," he barked. "Did you manage to get any paint on the actual set? This is a mess."

"It's almost all cleaned up," Ivy said. "No worries."

"That's a pretty lax attitude to have when your set looks like this two weeks before opening night," Parker said. "You think we have time to repaint everything? Do I need to take care of this for you?"

Miles jumped in, scratching a hand through the back of his hair as he looked up at the backdrop. "This? Just the primer coat," he said. "We're going to have it looking amazing in no time. Right, Howard?"

Three pairs of eyes turned to stare at me as I nodded. "The most amazing set ever," I said, cutting a hand through the air for emphasis. The wet sound of paint splattering caught my attention.

Forgot I was holding a paintbrush still. I winced at the sight of red paint sprinkled in an arc across the gym floor.

"Howard," Parker jerked his head to the side, "come here."

"He better not tell me to sit," I muttered.

"Be good," Ivy whispered at me as I dragged my feet over to where Parker waited. Helping out with the play was one thing. Taking orders from a snide fifteen-year-old with delusions of grandeur was another.

"Hey, bud." I stiffened up at the hand clasped on my shoulder. Parker's face was a mask of calm concern. "Looks like set-painting isn't really your thing either, is it?"

"It may not be my strongest skill set," I said, trying to squelch the urge to shrug out of his reach and failing.

"That's cool, that's cool." Parker nodded. "We'll find your thing. There's a little something for everyone in the theater."

If he tried to pat my head, I wasn't going to be held responsible for my actions.

"Could be that you weren't meant to be backstage," Parker said. "I know you like to play around at being a detective."

I gripped the paint brush in my hand, weighing the possible punishments against the satisfaction of smacking him with it.

"Maybe we should have put you on stage in the chorus or something. Let you show off that imagination," Parker mused. "Everyone fits in somewhere. That's the beauty of theater."

"I don't want the spotlight," I said through gritted teeth. "I'm happy to be helping my friends. Sorry about the mess. It won't happen again."

"I get it, but I'm not giving up. We'll figure you out yet, Howard. Now, go back and help your friends, bud." He shooed me away. "We gotta get this place cleaned up."

"Sure thing . . . bud." The force of my rage propelled me back over to Ivy and Miles at lightning speed. I held up a hand at the jokes dancing across both their faces. "Not one single word," I said.

"Wasn't going to say a thing, bud." Miles laughed.

"You gonna help us put this stuff away, bud?" Ivy started rolling up the last drop cloth, only slightly impeded by her shoulder-shaking snickers.

I sighed. "I hate you both."

Their cackles echoed around the gym as we finished putting everything away. Fifteen minutes later, we were out in the fresh air. I breathed deep, happy to get the smell of turpentine and smug high school freshman out of my nose.

"Everyone meeting us at Mrs. Hernandez's place?" Miles asked, and I nodded.

Ivy hopped along the sidewalk, dancing over the cracks, her bright green coat flaring out behind her. It had pineapples on it. I'd long given up on the idea of talking her into a stealthier piece of outerwear. "I hope they got the corner booth," she said.

I hummed in agreement, and she shot me with a sidelong look. "Broody McBrooderson, what's up? Mad about Parker knocking on your painting skills?"

"Maybe he's just mad about his lack of painting skills." Miles yelped as I kicked at the back of his knee.

Walking backward along the sidewalk in front me, Ivy shaded her eyes from the bright afternoon sun. Her sharp gaze softened as she saw through my sneer. "Howard," she said. "I know this may come as a shock to you, but you're not going to be awesome at everything you do. No one is."

"I'm pretty good at most things," Miles piped up from

behind us, and I counted the will to not push him off the sidewalk as one of my actual skills.

"Maybe you're not a behind-the-scenes kind of guy," Ivy said as we turned the corner onto Main Street. "You're good with people—"

Miles snorted and Ivy continued. "Maybe you can help with promo and ticket sales."

I mulled that idea over. I didn't really care what area I worked in as long as I was helping out somehow. The play was important to Ivy and I wanted to work with her to see it succeed. I'd do whatever was needed to because that's what partners did. You had each other's backs. Ivy had helped pull me out of more than one mess this year. I was ready to do whatever she needed. Even when it meant putting up with high-and-mighty high schoolers.

We walked up the steps to Mrs. Hernandez's café, and the tension began to bleed out of me inch by inch. On the other side of that door sat the rest of our crew, ready and waiting for our weekly agency meeting. I couldn't hold back the grin that started as we left the theater behind for more familiar territory: clients, criminals, and hopefully a stakeout or two.

Chapter Three

The bell chimed as we walked through the door, and we were instantly enveloped in the scent of fresh coffee and cookies.

"Guys, over here," a voice called out.

Ivy swung around and instantly pumped her fist. "Yessssss," she said. "Corner booth."

There was a flurry of activity as everyone shuffled around to make room. A full table was still a strange sight for me to see. Not too long ago, Wallace Investigations had been a one-man operation—I wouldn't even bother with a chair when I came in here. Just bellied up to the counter and chatted with Mrs. Hernandez over a slice of pie. Never felt the need to take up top real estate with a table for one. The shop had a cozy atmosphere and Mrs. H wasn't one to nudge people out the door. A fact I took shameless advantage of.

After Ivy came along, we became Wallace and Mason Investigations and our weekly meetings required room to spread out and strategize. We moved on to a table and, as the others joined in, grabbed a booth whenever we could. On a slow day, Mrs. H was even kind enough to reserve it. With our number at a steady six, the gesture was appreciated.

Miles folded his long limbs into the booth and did a complicated hand slap and shake with Carl Dean. Carl added some much-needed muscle to our gang and his poker face had come in handy on more than one occasion. Next to him was Ashi Jenkins, another former client and current band member who'd proven to be surprisingly good at stealth. Scotty Harris sat beside her and Ivy scooched in on their side. The worn leather of the seats creaked while everyone jammed in to fit together.

Mrs. Hernandez popped over with a heavily laden tray as I pulled up a chair. "What can I get for the latecomers?" she asked as she doled out drinks and baked goods.

"Hot chocolate, please," Ivy said.

"Me, too," Miles agreed.

"Coffee," I said. "Black."

"Three hot chocolates coming up." Mrs. Hernandez spun off with a wink. I once again found myself wondering if the cinnamon rolls of this establishment made up for the lack of respect for a man's beverage preferences.

"How'd you manage to beat us here from rehearsal?" Ivy asked Ashi as she snuck a hunk of muffin off of Scotty's plate.

Ashi giggled into her mug. "Not all of us had eight gallons of paint to clean up before we could leave."

Carl looked over at me. "They let you paint?"

"First of all, no one *let* me do anything," I said. "I helped and yes, there was a slight incident that took some time to clean up."

"How's the actual play going?" asked Scotty around a mouthful of cookie. "Hard to tell when I'm up to my ears in plant guts."

Ivy hummed as she tapped out a beat on the bright yellow table. "Okay," she said. "We need more practice. Feels like we've had more than our fair share of hiccups, but I think we're gonna be ready for next weekend. I'm more worried about getting all the props and stuff done."

"We can help again tomorrow," Ashi said and Scotty nodded.

"Are you sure?" Ivy darted a look between me and the

rest of the table. "I don't want to leave us short-handed for cases."

"We'll make a schedule," I said, waving away her worries. "Speaking of cases though, we've had a solid month and you'll be happy to know today is pay day." A small cheer went up around the table as I pulled out a stack of envelopes.

"Scotty, Ashi," I said, sliding two across the table to them. "Excellent work on the surveillance job last week. You guys have got eagle eyes."

Ashi grabbed her glasses by their bright green frames to wiggle them up and down her nose. "New prescription, for the win. I'm basically reverse Supergirl."

Scotty looked at her blankly.

"Because I have to keep my glasses on to have super powers? Never mind. Yay, pay day! Let's get more cookies."

Miles and Carl pocketed the envelopes I handed over. "Thanks for the assist on the Jones case," I said. "That could have gotten messy real fast without you guys backing me up."

I almost missed the frown that flit across Carl's face. "Problem, Carl? I divvied it up fair and square."

"Money's fine," Carl said. "It's—I signed up to investigate, not push people around. When am I going to do some of the real stuff?"

"Yeah," Miles chimed in. "All we do is assist or follow you around. When do we get a case of our own?"

"Don't underestimate your contributions," I said. "Kids needed help and you delivered. But I hear what you're saying." I pulled out my notebook as Ivy did the same. "What other cases do we have on the books?"

"Mine," Mrs. Hernandez said, plunking a mug down in front of me. Six pairs of eyes blinked at her in surprise as she dragged a chair over and sat down. "I think letting you take up a table for an hour every Friday should put me at the top of the list, yeah?"

"No arguments here," I said, tilting back in my chair. "What's been going on, Mrs. H?"

"The Business Association is up in arms." She sighed. "Someone's been, what do you kids call it? Tagging? They've been spray-painting all over the downtown. Some of it's not bad, but it's graffiti all the same. The police haven't managed to get anywhere and the BA wants to invest in a security system for all of the storefronts."

"Where do we come into play?" I asked, not quite connecting the dots.

"They want a top of the line, very expensive security system," she said. "All of the businesses would split the cost, but not all of us have that kind of money to throw around. I'd like to find our little artist before I have to pay up. Trust me: you're a much cheaper solution."

"I'm taking that as a compliment." I made eye contact with the team and they all nodded back. It was a no-brainer as far as cases went. Mrs. H was the best. Of course we'd help her out. "We'll start looking this weekend," I said. "Don't worry, Mrs. H. We've got it from here."

"I have no doubt that you do. I appreciate it." Her lips quirked before she rose from her spot. "Pleasure doing business with you, Howard."

I knocked off a small salute and sat up straight. "Only the best from Wallace and Mason Investigations."

"And Associates," Miles muttered.

I shot him a look. It was an old complaint, getting more tired by the second. Joining the team didn't mean you automatically got equal billing. Not that I didn't get where he was coming from—we all worked cases. Put in the time and effort. But that fact didn't bump my name off the top of the card. Or Ivy's. We earned it the hard way. Miles and the team had a long way to go before they earned it too. Months of blood, sweat, and detention that had gone into that letterhead. I had the permanent record to prove it. And when push came to shove, my name was the one people remembered. It was my name being passed along in the halls. The one people were learning to count on. It was my reputation to protect while Miles sat comfortably under the umbrella of "And Associates."

But the end of the day was not the time to argue about the details. "And Associates," I said, clinking my mug against his before turning to the rest of the table. Rubbing my hands together, I grinned at the spark of anticipation building in my gut. "Now, let's talk surveillance schedules." Everyone leaned in and we got to work.

Chapter Four

Half an hour later, Ivy and I were on our way home, walking down the shady streets of Grantleyville, enjoying the last bits of afternoon sun.

"You really don't mind that I can't help with any of the case work for the next couple weeks?" Ivy bumped her shoulder into mine.

"Eh, it's fine," I said, settling my well-worn brown fedora back into place. "You'll be back on the docket soon enough. We have more than enough people to cover. Too many. We should fire some of them."

"Howard." Ivy laughed. "You can't lie to me. I know you love having a whole band of detectives."

"First of all, I definitely wouldn't label them all as detectives and second of all, did you not see Carl steal the last of my cookie? That's grounds for dismissal right there."

"The cookie you swiped from Ashi?" My partner snorted.

"Fair point." That's what I got for leading by example. "You staying for dinner?" Ivy did a full-body scowl as we turned onto my street and I held my hands up. "Or not. Up to you."

"It's not that," she said, scrunching up her face. "My dad said I could hang out with you tonight in exchange for dinner with my mom Sunday night. They want us to eat together once a week 'as a family.'"

"Oh."

"Exactly."

We trudged up my driveway in silence. This was murky territory that I hadn't quite worked the map out to yet. Ivy's mom had left her and her dad early last year. They struggled along until the fall when they came to live with Ivy's grandma here in Grantleyville. After some adjustments, Ivy settled in and we'd become friends. Best friends. We had a routine and it was good. Until a few months ago, when Ivy's mom decided she was moving here to spend more time with Ivy. Things have been rocky and the topic was usually not open for discussion.

"Well, at least you're free now," I said. "And you'll be busy most of the weekend so it's just one dinner you have to worry about."

"It's never just the dinner," Ivy said darkly. "But you're right. We'll have fun tonight and then I can focus on all things theater." She flung open the side door on those last words and twirled into my house.

"Hang up your coats," Ma called from the kitchen. "Bags, too."

We dutifully followed her instructions as a door slammed above us and feet pounded down the stairs. "Is that Ivy?" my sister yelled out.

I groaned as my partner chuckled. An unfortunate side effect of Ivy sticking with Drama Club was that my theater-obsessed older sister thought they now had common ground. She felt compelled to talk to Ivy every time she came over. My friend Ivy. "I'm telling her you quit," I muttered.

"No," Ivy said as we wandered into the kitchen. "I like having someone to geek out over show stuff with. Her tolerance is much higher than yours."

"If you start talking about lighting arrangements again, I'm calling a time out."

My sister burst in from the dining room and immediately

grabbed hold of Ivy. "How was it today? Did you give Mrs. Pamuk the costume suggestions we talked about?"

"My day was great, Eileen," I said. "I'm so glad you asked."

"I know how your day went, Howeird." She set her face in a grimace. *"Tell me your alibi. What's a guy gotta do to get a clue around here? Gimme some more gum."*

"I can't decide if our parents should pay for more acting classes for you," I said, glaring at my sister. "Or cancel them."

Eileen wrinkled her nose at me. "Don't be rude. I promise I'll give you your friend back after dinner."

"Here," my mother stepped in between us, handing Ivy a stack of plates, "be a dear and start setting the table. I think it's best if you escape while you can."

Recognizing sound advice when she heard it, Ivy took the plates and ran. Ma rounded on the two of us. "Don't fight over the guest, children," she said. "It's rude."

"Ivy's not a guest," Eileen and I responded in unison.

"Well, we're not rude to family, either, so cut it out." She snapped a dish towel out of her pocket and tossed it at Eileen. "Sweetie, help me get the counters cleared up. Howard, please help Ivy finish off the table."

"I would love to go and help *my partner* with that job," I said. Eileen rolled her eyes as she followed Ma back to the sink. I grabbed utensils out of the drawer and got to work.

"Where's your dad?" Ivy looked up from adjusting plates on the table as I walked in.

"Picking up Blue," I said. "Time for her yearly checkup."

"Ah." Ivy nodded. "Getting all her shots and whatnot."

"More like a new chain and some rustproofing, but close enough." My ancient bike managed to keep chugging year after year, but a bit of TLC from the shop helped give her a little boost.

"Gotcha," Ivy said. "So it's like a little nip-and-tuck situation."

"Hey, now." I pointed a fork at my partner before setting it down. "Blue is beautiful just as she is. This is for health reasons only."

"I never said she wasn't. I'm glad she's getting some well-deserved pampering." Ivy straightened out the place settings I had put down and nodded at our handiwork. "I think we're good to go."

The side door slammed and Pops called out a greeting. Dinner was on the table in short order and Eileen and I managed to get through it without any major squabbles.

"Do you need a ride home tonight, Ivy?" Ma asked as we started clearing away the dishes.

"No, thanks," Ivy said. "My dad's going to come pick me up in a bit."

I jerked my chin toward the back door. "Want to go say hi to Blue and hang out in the office?"

"Definitely." Ivy wiped her hands on a napkin and grinned at my folks. "Thanks for dinner, Mrs. Wallace. It was great."

Pops looked up from loading the dishwasher. "See you soon, Ivy."

"You're welcome any time," Ma said, waving us out of the kitchen.

We grabbed our coats and headed out to the garage. Blue was in her usual corner, propped up on her kickstand, looking shiny and new.

"Blue!" Ivy pressed a hand to her heart. "I barely recognized you." She reached out to pat Blue's handlebars. "Clean up nicely, don't you, girl?"

I grinned at Blue's creaks, touching a toe to her front tire. "Little buff here and there, little bit of grease, and you're good to go, right, Blue?" Rearranging the blanket over her seat, I made sure to tug the corners over her back wheel. "I think she's got a few more years left in her."

Ivy stepped back as we made our way back out into the yard. "I should get a bike," she said.

"What happened to your scooter?"

"Nothing," she said. "I just think I should find something with a little more pizzazz, you know?"

I squinted at my partner.

Ivy squinted back. "What?"

"I'm trying to picture you with *more* pizzazz."

"You know what I mean." Ivy batted at my shoulder. "I want my own Blue."

"You want a semi-possessed bike that runs with a mind of its own and gives you attitude at every turn?" Hauling open the door to the office, I breathed in the dusty air, happy to be back in our own space after being forced to spend the winter months in the garage. I ignored the slight lean as the whole structure followed the motion. *Building* was too generous a word. Considering it was little more than a few boards held together with nails, paint, and misplaced confidence, I offered up the usual silent thanks when the entire mess didn't come toppling down.

"Yes," Ivy said brightly. "Exactly."

"We'll call Gary's Bike Shop this weekend and see if they have any beasts that fit the bill."

"Cool." My partner flopped down into the stinky, comfy

chair, lifting her legs up over the arm. "It'd be nice to have a better set of wheels to get around town on. Not have to rely on Dad and Grandma so much."

I frowned as I sat in the rickety chair behind the desk. "They putting up a fuss?"

"No," Ivy said. "But, every car ride turns into an opportunity to talk. Child locks go down. Concerned adult voice comes on. It's a bit much."

"We'll look into it," I promised. My sympathy ran deep, having endured more than my own fair share of parental *talks.* "Get you set up in no time."

"Oh! We could go on Sunday and then you could come over for dinner!"

"The dinner with your mom dinner?" I was shaking my head no before I could even finish the sentence. Hard pass. Ivy's mom and I had crossed paths one time and that was enough for me. For her too as far as I could tell. "I don't think we're at the break bread stage of our relationship considering the fact that she hates me."

"She doesn't hate you," Ivy said automatically and I raised an eyebrow at her. Her mom had repeatedly asked how I knew Ivy and kept calling me Harold. And then started grilling Ivy on whether or not she'd made any friends since she moved here.

"She's not your biggest fan," Ivy said. "But we don't care what she thinks and it'll be way better if you're there. Please, Howard?"

Partnership meant having each other's backs, I reminded myself. "Yeah, okay," I said. "As long as my folks agree."

A horn sounded from the driveway and Ivy sighed. "That's me." She rolled out of the chair and headed for the door. "Thanks, Howard. I know it won't be fun, but at least now it won't completely suck. Talk to you after rehearsal tomorrow?"

I walked her out to the drive. "Sounds good." Watching the tail lights disappear, I popped my head in the garage to say goodnight to my ride. Patting Blue's handlebars, I hopped up onto the shelf beside her. "Well, Blue," I said, scratching her headlamp. "We've got a day and a half to figure out how I'm going to charm my way through dinner with Ivy's mom."

Blue creaked in her corner.

"What do you mean I should cancel?"

Chapter Five

The insistent ringing of my alarm jolted me out of the depths of unconsciousness. Scratching at sleep-encrusted eyes with one hand, I slapped the other down, sending my clock crashing to the floor. A smile tugged at my mouth as I reveled in the silence. Nothing like starting the day out with a swift serving of justice.

I sat bolt upright in bed, remembering what day it was.

Saturday. The prime workday for Wallace and Mason Investigations. I had walls to inspect and a vandal to track.

I threw my lucky coat over my shoulder and headed down to the kitchen. Despite its "most important meal of the day" status, breakfast was a slapdash affair in the Wallace household. I slapped some peanut butter on a piece of bread and prepared to dash, when Pops staggered into the room.

"Coffee," he muttered. I stepped out of the way as he lurched to the coffee maker. I came by my early-morning reticence honestly. Scalding hot caffeine in hand, Pops pulled up a stool and inhaled the fumes over the kitchen counter. His eyes focused on me after the first sip. "Mmm," he said, wits quickly gathering. "Howard. Laundry?"

"Very nearly put away," I said, grabbing my own mug out of the cabinet. Ma wandered in just as I had it filled to the brim, snatching the cup out of my hand.

"Very thoughtful. Thank you, sweetie," she said, taking a small sip and making a face. "Needs a little something." She poured a small mountain of sugar into the mug before nodding in satisfaction.

"Where are you off to?" Ma asked as she took in my work clothes and the to-go breakfast I was cramming into my mouth.

"Caught a new case yesterday," I said after gulping down a chunk of bread. "Mrs. H has a graffiti problem. Gonna check it out, help her shut it down."

"Home in time for dinner," she said, the lack of question mark clear in her tone.

I knocked off a salute and headed out the door as Pop

mumbled his good-bye. Making my way into the garage, I grinned at the sight of my ride already up and raring to go. It had been a long, cold winter and Big Blue never took well to being cooped up.

"Come on, girl," I said, wheeling her down the driveway. "We've got a big day ahead and more than enough ground to cover."

Blue and I coasted along the sidewalk, making it downtown to Mrs. H's well before the rest of the crew. Well, almost.

I hit the brakes at the sight of Leyla Bashir snapping photos of the doodles decorating the coffee shop's wall. Leyla was the editor of the Grantleyville Middle School blog. She'd covered the dognapping case we worked a few months ago and her story blew up big time. Now she was more determined than ever to catch the next big scoop.

"Leyla," I said with a nod. "To what do I owe the pleasure?"

"Word on the street is we have a graffiti bandit on the loose," she said, lowering her phone to hit me with a sideways look. "People need to know if their property is in danger."

"Word travels fast, but it's not always true. Who said anything about danger?"

"The word I get is always true," Leyla said. "And let's not minimize the situation. I'd rather talk business."

"You up for the usual?" Since working together in February, Leyla and I had come to a mutually beneficial arrangement. I gave her the inside track on any newsworthy cases I took on and she passed along any juicy tidbits she discovered on her beat. Having an extra set of eyes on the graffiti case wouldn't hurt.

She brushed a chunk of her blue bangs off to the side and squinted at me. "You get an hour lead-time on anything I find," she said. "Twenty minutes if it's something big. I get to post whatever I find no matter how it affects your case. And no sitting on info on your end." Leyla jabbed a finger at my chest. "I don't want to find out you left me hanging."

"Would you like my firstborn child as well?"

"I don't do payment plans," Leyla said.

"You'd think we haven't gone over this arrangement a time or two hundred," I said, rolling my eyes.

"Never assume a deal carries over, Howard." She smirked at me. "Who knows what you'd try to get away with if the parameters weren't clear."

I spluttered at that. "Because I'm the shady one in this situation."

"You're not *not* shady." Leyla and I spun around at the new voice and met Carl and Miles as they strolled up.

"Appreciate the back-up, as always, Miles," I said, glancing at my watch. "Five minutes earlier and you're right on time." Pulling out a pack of Juicy Smash, I popped out a piece before handing the pack over to Carl.

"What's the plan?" Carl jerked a nod at the graffiti covered wall.

"Miles, take some pictures of this for our own records. Carl, you and I are going to start canvassing the street. We need to nail down what stores have been hit and when. Find a pattern, get a bead on who's next. Leyla—"

"Is in charge of her own schedule, thank you very much." Leyla took one last shot of the wall and slipped her phone back in her bag. "I have my own leads to chase down. Remember our agreement, Howard Wallace. Keep in touch." She strode down the sidewalk without another word.

Straightening the collar of my lucky coat, I gave a sharp nod to my crew. "Let's go."

Canvassing was grunt-work—slow and relentlessly menial with the added frustration of door after door getting slammed in our faces. It was necessary to any investigation though. Something that may seem insignificant to the person who spotted it could crack a case wide open. But first you had to convince people to talk to you—and that meant pulling out the patented Wallace charm.

....-.. .- ... -   -... --- .-

"You want paint all over your walls, fine!" I hollered over my shoulder as two hands pushed me firmly out of the hardware store. Carl stood waiting on the sidewalk, catching one of my sleeves before I stumbled into the street.

"No clues at Grantley Hardware?" He raised an impassive brow as he waited for me to right myself.

"They did not have any information to offer at this time," I said, tightening the belt on my coat. None of the Grantley-owned business had anything to share. I'd gone in, ready to glad-hand my way into some intel, but they weren't having any of it. Apparently, shelling out big bucks for a security system held more appeal than chatting it up with the local P.I.s. Pompous jerks. So much for community spirit.

"There's Miles," Carl said. "Want to see how he's making out and compare notes?"

"Doubt he's doing much better than us," I grumbled.

Carl squinted as he watched Miles approach. "Think you might be right about that."

I looked closer at Miles as we crossed the street. He had a hand pressed into his side and was hunched over. "Hey," he said, panting. "Hey, guys."

Carl looked him up and down, a slight frown creasing his forehead. "Breathe."

"What's wrong with you?" I helped him lean against the nearest wall. "Someone run you out of their store too?"

"Was in pursuit," Miles said. "Thought I saw a suspicious looking guy. Chased him."

This was the problem with working with people. They came up with ideas. On their own. "Why would you do that? Why didn't you call for help?" I demanded. We had procedures in place for a reason. "What made this guy suspicious? How did chasing him help?"

"I thought I could catch him. There wasn't any time. He was lurky-looking. And again, I thought I could catch him and at least ask some questions." Miles stood up, breathing easy enough to blow a bit of sass into his words.

"Did you try asking questions before you starting chasing him?" One look at Miles's face answered that question. "All right. No more splitting up. We'll tackle the rest of the street as a team. And no more talking." Carl nodded and Miles muttered to himself.

"Carl, you're doing a great job," I said. "Keep it up."

"Howard!"

Ah. The dulcet tones of a voice filtered through eighty-plus years of cigarettes and bad coffee. I'd recognize it anywhere. "Marvin," I said, spinning around.

The wizened owner of our local pawnshop stood on his front stoop, waving us over with a liver-spotted claw. Both Marvin and his shop were Grantleyville institutions. Long-standing enough to be respected, worn enough to be an eyesore, and ancient enough not to care. "I'm too old to be cavorting around sidewalks," he said. "Enjoy your youth and use your legs. Come on, already."

We walked over to the cracked front steps of Marvin's on Main at an unimpressive speed if the snapping fingers were any indication. I tipped my hat at Marvin. "You hollered?"

"Just the man I wanted to see." He took a quick look around the street before leaning in close. "Word is you're working Alva's case. Tracking down the doodler?" I nodded and he cackled with a note of grim satisfaction. "She's a smart one. Getting out of the Grantley surveillance scam before it gets off the ground. Okay, come with me." Marvin hustled down the steps, herding us with pokes of a bony finger until we came around the side of his building.

I peered down the cluttered alley before digging in my heels. "Any context for this field trip, Marv?"

"I've been hit." He pointed at the brick wall and spat in

disgust. "This masterpiece was done sometime this morning. Chuck Grantley popped his head in the shop first thing to make sure I knew about it. Smug little—"

"We should take a closer look at this," I said, hauling Miles and Carl up to the wall with me. The faded yellow bricks were peppered with grime and bits of crawling ivy, but the overall dinginess only made the spray-painted artwork stand out in stark relief. I tilted my head as I took in the swooping lines and messy drips. "Is that supposed to be you?"

"Got it in one." Marvin tapped at his nose. "Now show me why you earn the big bucks and figure out who put it there. I'm going in with Mrs. H. You can make it a joint case."

"Doesn't mean you get to pay half the fee," I said.

Marvin hacked out a laugh before sobering quickly. "We're counting on you, Howard. You're the only one I trust on this. The only guy for the job."

"Uncle Marv," Carl said as Miles made a noise of protest. "Standing right here."

"Right, right," Marvin said. "You should help too. All hands on deck."

Miles looked ready to burst while Carl shook his head at his uncle. "We've got a great crew, Marvin. In fact," I said, thinking back to yesterday's meeting, "I'm going to put Miles and Carl in charge of your case. They're more than capable of handling it."

Marvin looked dubious as he thought that over. "As long as you're checking up on them," he said. "And when you catch this punk, you bring 'em straight to me."

We spit in our hands and shook on it. Miles jumped in immediately after. "Don't you worry, Mr. Parsons," he said, whipping out a tissue before pumping Marvin's hand up and down. "We will track this criminal down and bring him or her to justice. That's an agency guarantee."

I dragged a hand down my face, biting back a sigh.

"Howard." Marvin stared at me. "What."

"Stop talking," I said to Miles. "Be in touch, Marvin." Grabbing Miles by the sleeve, I towed him out to the sidewalk. Carl said a quick good-bye to his uncle and followed suit.

"Howard, hands off. Calm down." Miles yanked his arm out of my grasp. "What is wrong with you?"

"Could ask you the same question. How many times have I told you to follow a client's lead? You know how deals with Marvin work. A tissue, Miles? Really? That's just rude." I closed my eyes and counted to five. "Guess I should be happy you left your hand sanitizer at home this time," I sighed.

My eyes flew open at the sound of a lid snicking open. Miles quickly stuffed his hands back in his pocket, refusing to meet my stare.

"To be fair," Carl said, rubbing his hands together. "We were just in an alley."

"If you guys are going to take this case on," I said. "I need to know that you can handle it. You're representing the agency. You ready for that responsibility?"

"We are all over this, Howard," Miles said. "We will make a plan and we will make you proud." The doubt must have shown on my face. His eagerness began to fade before his eyes lit up again. Miles brought his hand up to spit in it before holding it out. "We're going to solve this case, I promise."

I exchanged a quick look with Carl who stared back steadily as he also spit in his hand. They stood there patiently, hands out, until I spit into my own hand, reached over and shook theirs one at a time.

"Still so gross," Miles said.

"I think we're done for today. Meet me at the same time tomorrow and we'll finish our interviews, see what we can pull together." We parted ways and I headed home with Blue. Plenty of daylight left to burn and cases to work without interruption.

....-.. .- ...   - -... --- .-

"Howard, phone!"

My sister's scream carried across the back yard in through the open door of the home office. Pinning one last tack on my map, I stood back to look at my progress. A decent chunk of the graffiti targets were confirmed—now I had to figure out the pattern. Easy peasy.

"It's Ivy. I'm walking away. Come talk to your friend, you weirdo." The back door slammed shut. Not wanting to leave my partner hanging, I shoved my files in the cabinet and headed out to the house, door loosely locking behind me.

My mother was lecturing Eileen as I walked through the kitchen. "When I say let Howard know the phone is for him, I mean walk out the door and go to his shed—"

"Office." I corrected as I picked the phone up off the table. Ignoring Eileen when she pooh-poohed the semantics, I headed up to my room. "Hey, Ivy."

"You know, if you'd manage to keep your cell phone privileges, we could avoid productions like this," she said. "I think Eileen damaged my ear drum."

"Convince my parents that using it for surveillance is not a groundable offense and we can make that happen."

She snorted at that. "How'd it go with the guys today?"

I flopped down on my bed and dragged a hand down my face. "We're like a well-oiled machine at this point."

Ivy patiently waited out that half-truth at her end of the line.

"Like a well-oiled machine that keeps using too much oil and is sliding and tripping all over the place. And bits keep falling off and having to be taped back on and now there's tape in places where no tape should ever be—" I took a deep breath.

"That good, eh?"

I laughed half-heartedly at that. "It's gonna take some work. That's it. We're a work-in-progress."

"They need time to learn," Ivy said. "You weren't the best detective either right off the bat."

"Lies."

"Really." I could feel the phone trying to turn over in my hand with the force of Ivy's eye roll. "Do we need to go over the Howard's greatest mistakes highlight reel?"

"At least they're great. Moving on, how was *your* day?"

"You know you don't get points for asking about my stuff if it's just because you don't want to talk about your stuff."

"I want to know," I said. "I've been swimming in cases all day. Tell me about rehearsal. Who's fixing my paint job?"

Ivy scoffed. "Scotty, the poor guy. I thought he was going to cry when we handed him the paint brush." She trailed off.

"And?" I prompted when she failed to continue.

"Rehearsal was weird? Like weirder than normal which is saying something."

"Weird how?" I asked, sitting up on my bed. This conversational turn required more serious posture.

"It's a lot to explain and it's probably nothing," Ivy said. "You're busy with cases. Don't worry about it."

"Ivy. Tell me."

"I think," she said, drawing out the pause. "There's something peculiar going on."

"I love peculiar," I said. "It's my favorite branch of weird."

Ivy barked out a laugh. "Okay, fine, but I still want to talk about it in person. I think we're going to need charts."

"You have to go see a man about a bike anyway. We'll make a day of it. New wheels and case charts. Doesn't get better than that."

We made plans to meet up in the morning and said goodnight. Taking a minute to visualize my office, I grinned. Between the vandalism maps and upcoming charts of peculiarities, we were well on our way to covering up the rest of the wall gaps. All in a day's work.

Chapter Six

I f you'd asked me who was the best set of wheels in Grant-leyville, I'd say Big Blue, hands down, every time. She didn't have flash or style or . . . speed, but there was an aura of mystery about her that went beyond wondering how she stayed in one piece. A certain sense of magic that came with extreme age. Big Blue had the title on lock. Until today.

I let out a low whistle as I looked over the bike my partner had picked out. Mottled green paint from tip to tail finished off with faded chrome fenders. A sturdier build I'd never seen — the whole thing probably weighed more than Ivy. A small shelf was jimmy-rigged to the back with a plastic carton strapped to it. Gotta love a model that came with storage. "She's a beaut, Ivy."

Ivy grinned broadly as she patted the handlebars. "Her name is Tank."

"I believe it."

"This is the bike you want?" Mr. Mason looked Tank up and down doubtfully. "I think you'll need a stool to get on it. What if you fall over? It could crush you. It looks like it should have a motor."

"This is the one, Dad," Ivy said. "We've already bonded."

"I—Okay," Mr. Mason said. "I'm going to go talk to Gary about safety gear."

Concluding our business at the bike shop, I unlocked Blue, we said our good-byes to Mr. Mason, and we headed back to the home office. Ivy and Tank had a few false starts as Ivy tried to get enough power going to move her brute of a machine. Once she built up some steam, they wobbled down the sidewalk well enough. Blue gave them a reasonably wide berth. "I'd hold off taking Tank down any hills for the time being."

"Everything's fine!"

"Tree, Ivy," I called out. "Tree!"

"Still fine!"

....-.. .- ...   - -... --- .-

We made it to the home office in one piece, leaving Blue and Tank to recuperate in the garage. I retrieved the latest files out of the cabinet as my partner geared up to give me the lowdown on the play.

"I don't like it, Howard." Ivy kicked at a book and sent it skidding across the office floor. She threw herself down in the ugly comfy chair and scowled. "Something peculiar is going on and I don't like it."

Crouching by my desk, I tugged out the much-abused tome and dusted it off on my lucky coat. "Much as I respect your right to vent your frustrations," I said, setting the book back on the shelf. "Please try to avoid venting them on the training materials."

"Augh." My partner groaned, half upside down in the chair, with one leg slung over the back and the other over the patched arm. "I'm sorry, but everything is terrible and I'm dying. That book has nothing on my pain."

I dropped down into my chair and bit back a laugh. "Something rotten in the GMS Drama Club?"

"More rotten than Parker's acting," Ivy sniped. She dragged a hand over her face and sighed. "I don't know what's going on. It's like, everything that can go wrong has gone wrong. Nothing huge, but it never ends. Like I said, pe*culiar*."

"What kind of stuff?" I grabbed my notebook.

"Missing scripts, wrong paint color for the set—" she started listing things off.

"No offense, but that doesn't sound unusual for a middle school drama production," I said.

"Full offense!" Ivy wriggled her way back into an upright position. "Okay, that's a lie, but seriously, the lack of skill level to incident ratio does not compute. We may be amateurs, but we're not idiots."

I leaned back in my chair and pondered the options. "Ruling out operator error, which we haven't entirely," I said, shooting Ivy a look. "We're left with what? Someone deliberately messing things up?"

Ivy threw her arms out to the room at large. "Nothing more *peculiar* than sabotage!"

"I feel like we're overusing peculiar. Can we pick a different word?"

"Yes, we've moved on to sabotage, keep up." My partner was already pacing the floor, brain gears turning at top speed.

"Sabotage is a pretty hefty accusation to toss around, Ivy," I said. "You can't use it in a fishing expedition. We need solid proof to back it up."

Ivy stopped in her tracks and stared at me, chewing at

her bottom lip. "You believe me? That something weird is going on?"

"Of course I believe you." You get far enough into a partnership, you trust their gut as well as your own. "I'm saying we need to put the work in first."

"You guys are already working a ton of cases and I've been off the roster with the play and it's probably—"

"Ivy." I held up a hand to cut off the rant. "We can handle checking this out. I gave the graffiti case to Miles and Carl—"

"You did what?" Ivy grinned at me. "Did they lose their minds? How excited are they? Look at you. Delegating."

"I'm keeping an eye on them, but yeah, they're taking point," I said. Still not entirely sure that was the right decision.

Ivy chewed on her lip. "Are you okay with it? Maybe you should be sticking with them? I could be overthinking the play stuff."

"We can handle it," I said. "They won't be completely on their own, but it frees me up to look into your case. It's important. We'll make it happen."

She let out a sigh as her shoulders sagged in relief. "Okay," she said. "Okay, that's good. Thanks, Howard."

"Don't thank me yet," I said, taping paper to the wall. "Let's get this figured out first. Start from the beginning."

Ivy picked up a pen and launched into the timeline. "Little things at the start. Stuff going missing and then miraculously turning up. Fine, not out of the ordinary. Kids lose their scripts every year so no one really questioned it. The first few times. Then all the permission slips for weekend rehearsal were lost which was a pretty big deal."

I jotted down notes, sorting the information into my mental files as she spoke.

"Mrs. Grantley-Smythe, uh, Pricilla Grantley-Smythe, I think? She's one of the office admins—she tracked them down," Ivy said. "Someone put them in an outbox instead of an inbox or something."

"Is this the same Mrs. Grantley-Smythe who's volunteering with the play?" I added her name to the side of our timeline.

"Yup," Ivy said. "She's on the board of the Parents' Association and they offered to have someone help Mrs. Pamuk with the production. I think it's an excuse to have eyes and ears on the ground. Protecting their investment."

Back in February, our big dognapping case ended up revealing a scheme funneling money from the arts programs at school into the sports teams. Leyla helped bust that story wide open and it landed the Parents' Association and the school with some serious questions to answer. Dropping a load of money on the school musical was one of their answers. But nothing came without strings.

"Makes sense," I said, tapping at the paper. "What else?"

"All the music got wiped from Mrs. Pamuk's laptop this week. Parker was able to get it back. It had all been specially cut so it would've been a pain to redo."

"Thank goodness for Parker," I said, marking down his name.

"He certainly thinks so," Ivy said. "Now, yesterday—yesterday was the kicker. We go to the senior center for rehearsal and someone had cancelled our booking."

I turned to face my partner. "*That's* peculiar."

"Right?" Ivy's eyes widened as she nodded furiously. "Parker was arguing with the front desk, sort of making progress, when Mrs. Grantley-Smythe swept in and dropped the G Card. The shuffleboard crew had already stolen our space so we had to use one of the teeny rooms, but we made it work."

"They had no record of who cancelled it?"

"Nope, just a couple of thick black lines wiping out our slot," Ivy said.

We took a step back to look at the board. "Increasing in

severity the closer we get to opening night," I said, tracing a finger down the timeline. "Who do we like for main players?"

"Well, Parker and Mrs. Grantley-Smythe have been involved in solving most of the problems and Mrs. Pamuk and Nina, our stage manager, have discovered most of them."

"And finding or solving problems doesn't mean you didn't cause them," I said.

"Exactly." Ivy added the last two names onto the list. "How do you want to tackle this?"

"I'll come to rehearsal tomorrow to help out and try to get a better read on these guys. See what I can sniff out."

"We'll have to find you a better cover," Ivy said. "No one's going to let you near the set after Friday."

"A guy tries to help out his friends and all he gets is grief," I moaned.

Ivy cackled as she put the pens away. "Hey, speaking of helping out your friends, today is Sunday."

"Mm-hm." I plopped down in my chair and put my feet up on the desk. I knew where this conversation was going and I was getting comfortable before it progressed any further.

"You must be getting pretty hungry." My partner rocked back on her heels, eyeing me sideways.

"I could eat."

"Howard, come on." Ivy shoved my feet off the desk and hopped up in their place. "Sunday dinner. You said you'd go."

"That was a thing that I said." I rolled my eyes as Ivy did a fist-pump. "But if your mom rags on my coat again, I'm out of there."

"Totally understood," Ivy said. "But it will be fine, I swear."

....-.. .- ... - -... --- .-

"Howard." Ivy's mom walked up as we came in through the front door. "I didn't realize you were joining us tonight. Please, let me take your . . . coat."

I shot a look at Ivy and she grimaced at me, mouthing *sorry*. Shrugging off my coat and any implied insults, I smiled. As far as first shots fired went, it was fairly mild. I could handle this. For Ivy's sake.

"Smells great, Lillian," I called out to Ivy's grandma as I entered the kitchen.

"Howard!" She waved at me from the stove. "Just in time to set the table. You know where everything is."

Ivy and I grabbed what was needed and had everything ready to go as Lillian brought out a mouth-watering plate of enchiladas to the table. Once everyone was seated, I dug in. Better to have my mouth full than have to answer awkward questions from Ivy's mom. A strategy that wasn't helping my partner at all.

"How's school?" Ivy's mom asked. "Did you finish all of your homework before you went over to Howard's today?"

Ivy made a few humming noises, then held up a finger before pointing at her cheeks, stuffed chipmunk-style, with a helpless shrug.

"How is the play going? Are you keeping up with everything? I don't see how you could possibly have time to be helping Howard with his little *hobby* with what you have on your plate. School is the priority, you know." Ivy's mom was in fine form today.

"Bianca," Ivy's dad said with a hint of warning in his voice.

"What? I'm not allowed to ask how my daughter is spending her time?"

I took a deep drink of water as Ivy eyed the exits. Time to step in and do my duty as partner and friend.

"You are correct, Bianca. Uh, Mrs. Mason," I said, changing gears when she narrowed her eyes at me. "Ivy's mom? Moving on." I cleared my throat as Ivy sunk down in her chair. "Ivy has had quite a bit on her schedule lately so she's on a bit of a hiatus from the agency. Which is great news for the play and all of her homework, obviously. But don't worry about my hobby that is actually a very viable business. We have some adequate team members now who have been helping out with the caseload."

"And your parents are okay with you running all over town sticking your nose in other people's business?"

"Mom!" Ivy gasped.

"My parents are fine with it," I said. "They're around pretty regularly so they actually know what I'm up to."

Mrs. Mason's lips thinned out in a tense line.

Lillian coughed, dabbing at her mouth with a napkin. "Didn't your father help you out with a few cases when you started out?"

"He did," I said. "Funny story about a lost dog." I forged ahead, recounting some of the highlights in as much detail that wasn't legally binding as I could. Lillian and Mr. Mason played along, laughing and gasping at all the appropriate places. We managed to get through the meal without further interrogation. Mrs. Mason didn't contribute much else to the conversation which was fine by me. Fine by everyone else too it seemed. Dessert came around and Lillian plopped a double scoop of ice cream in front of me with a wink.

After wolfing down my bowl full of frozen mint-chocolate goodness, I headed home. Between her mom and the play, Ivy had more than enough on her plate these days. It was the right move to put Miles and Carl on the graffiti case. My partner needed me more. I might not be able to paint sets, but I could look into the odd action going on behind the scenes. We'd get to the bottom of it and give her a chance to focus back on having fun.

I pulled into the garage, ready to do some focusing of my own. With multiple jobs on the go the only way to keep things straight was to keep it fresh. After tucking Blue in, I stepped into the home office for one last look at the boards. They were overflowing with facts and suspects. It was a staggeringly different sight from the stark walls of less than a year ago.

Nope. I smiled to myself. Definitely not a hobby.

Chapter Seven

Monday morning announced its arrival with the usual amount of exuberance. A ray of sunlight snuck through a crack in the curtains to pierce through my eyelids, forcing me out of a peaceful slumber.

"Who's a guy gotta bribe to get boards on his windows?" I grumbled as I dragged back the covers and hauled myself out of bed. Twenty minutes of stumbling around my house later, I grabbed my bag and went out to get Blue.

"Hey there, partner." Ivy and Tank were turning lazy circles on the drive, looking far too perky for such an early hour.

I mumbled out a greeting on my way to the garage. Blue was lounging in her spot, kickstand down, head lamp out. She looked about as ready for the morning's run as I felt.

"Up and at 'em, Blue," I said.

No response.

"Come on, girl. Ivy and Tank are waiting."

That got her going enough for us to wheel outside in time to hear Ivy explaining to Tank why some friends were morning people and some weren't.

"And there's no shame in it, Tank," I said, shaking a finger at the pair of them. "No shame. Mornings are meant for sleeping in and breakfast foods. This walking around and talking business is just unnatural."

Blue let out a ladylike creak of agreement.

Ivy placed her hands over Tank's handlebars. "Don't listen, Tank. They're a bad influence."

"Bad influence," I said as Blue and I rolled down to the sidewalk. "Or trailblazing role models?"

"Can you technically blaze any trail at that speed?" Ivy smirked, swooping by on Tank. "Asking for a friend."

"Speed has nothing to do with it," I shouted after her disappearing taillight.

Ivy was locking her ride up to the bike rack when Blue and I finally puffed our way onto the schoolyard. They both looked entirely too smug.

"Laugh it up, Tank," I said. "You're the one who's going to

be stuck next to a cranky Blue all day." With a sharp snap, I clicked my lock into place and patted Blue's seat before heading inside.

We were on the short side of punctual today and had to hustle to make it to homeroom. Tuning out the crackle of morning announcements, I settled into my seat and snuck a quick peek at the clock. Only a few hours until lunch.

Then the real workday could begin.

....-.. .- ... - -... --- .-

"Look at this," Carl said, frowning over our notes. We'd annexed a lunch table in order to spread out and look at our info properly. The general chaos of the caf was a perfect shield. No one ever gave our group a second look.

Carl passed the notebooks over to me. "Every business owner said that they noticed the graffiti before 9 a.m. and after 4 p.m."

"Nothing during the day," Miles said. "And nothing overnight."

I mulled that over as I chewed through a mouthful of raisins.

"So our suspect is someone who's busy during the day and doesn't prowl around at night. Odds are pretty good it's a kid, given the nature of the crime," I said. "At least we don't have to worry about a late-night stakeout. Now we have to get a step ahead."

"How so?" Miles asked.

I flipped open one of the notebooks to a fresh page and sketched out a quick map of the downtown. "Here's all of the places they've hit so far," I said, marking each spot with a circle. "They're jumping around, trying to keep things random, but they've hit Grantley Convenience three times." I put three *x*'s on that location. "The question is why?"

Miles read over his notes. "They painted over the graffiti," he said. "They were the only ones and the perp came back each time."

"Didn't appreciate having their work tampered with," Carl said.

"We can use that." I nodded. "Use Marvin's place to set a trap. Carl, call Marv and let him know we need some paint and supplies. You and Miles can head there after school and paint over the artwork. Ferret out a good surveillance spot while you're at it."

"We know how to run a stakeout, Howard," Miles said.

"Good, good, good," Ivy said, elbowing Miles out of his seat, forcing him to move further down the table. "Time for new business. Let's talk about my case."

She spread the notes we'd hammered out on Sunday down on the table. "I think we can all agree that something strange is going on with the play."

Ashi, Scotty, Carl, and Miles nodded, moving in closer.

"The field of suspects right now is wide," she said. "Too wide. We need to narrow it down."

"Miles and Carl are out, but the rest of us can work the rehearsals." I tapped a finger on our list of names. "Four suspects and four of us. Pick a person and track them, but keep your distance. We don't want anyone getting wise."

"If you see anything weird go down," Ivy said, "you come and tell us immediately."

Assignments distributed, we wrapped up our meeting in time to finish lunch.

Two cases of simple surveillance.

This was going to be no problem.

Chapter Eight

It was a big problem.

Monday rolled into Tuesday and both of our cases were dead in the water. Miles and Carl painted over Marvin's wall and picked a post with a clear line of sight across the street. The diner let them keep their window table as long as they kept ordering.

Twenty dollars later, they'd yet to catch a glimpse of our perp. Good thing we were charging Marvin and Mrs. H expenses. I was doing my best to give them room to operate, a little space to figure things out on their own, but another part of me itched to head down there and take charge. I couldn't help wondering if there was something they were missing. Something my more experienced eyes would catch.

Except my eyes weren't faring any better on Ivy's case. Monday's rehearsal had passed without incident, and I was mostly flying solo. Ivy, Scotty, and Ashi had their roles in the play to attend to which meant keeping an eye on our suspects fell into second place. We'd yet to catch anyone in the act of doing anything. It was getting on my nerves.

Tuesday afternoon found me entering the gym in a foul mood. "Something blatantly suspicious," I muttered to myself. "Something I can follow up on, that's all I ask."

My ears perked up at the sound of Scotty in hysterics. Finally. I barreled across the room to see what the fuss was about. Ivy and Ashi were holding Scotty back from his work table. It was collapsed on the ground with two legs lying under it. Scotty's project was in a dented heap on the floor, the paper crushed and wires bent beyond repair.

"Audrey II!" Scotty cried. "How did this happen?"

Excellent question. I pulled my partner aside for a consult. "Like this when you came in?" I murmured to Ivy.

She nodded, pulling out a pack of Juicy Smash. "Scotty swears everything was secured when he checked on it this morning," she said, popping a piece in her mouth and tossing me the pack. "Legs giving out on the table could have happened on their own, but the level of smushedness on that plant did not."

I leaned around Ivy to peer at the green mess Scotty was trying to put back together. "Think someone stomped on poor old Angela?"

"*Audrey*," Ivy said. "And yes, looks like."

Ivy and I set the table back to rights as Ashi helped Scotty pull the remains of Audrey II up off the floor. Scotty looked over the mishmash of parts with a groan. "I'm never going to fix this."

"Oh, no!" Mrs. Pamuk and Parker had arrived to see what the commotion was about. "Scotty, all of your hard work," Mrs. Pamuk said. "I'm so sorry. Can you work with this and put it back together? Or do you think we need to start again from scratch?"

"I don't know," Scotty said, head hung mournfully, hands clutching at his tufts of blond hair. "Is it possible to rebuild your heart?"

"We're gonna try, big guy." Parker clapped a hand on Scotty's shoulder. "I don't think it's as bad as it looks. We can sort this out, Mrs. P."

"Are you sure?" She looked back and forth from Scotty to the table, a worried line digging in between her brows. "Would some extra hands help?"

A chunk of green fabric fluttered to the ground, and Scotty sighed. "We'll need more stuff," he said.

"I'll see what I can do with the budget," Mrs. Pamuk said. "Hopefully I can pick up more fabric tonight."

"See? It's not so bad," Parker said, bumping Scotty with his elbow. "There was no budget back in my day. Something like this happened, you had to throw some glue on it and hope for the best." He tilted his head with a shrug. "If you had any glue left that is."

Scotty poked at the crushed chicken wire and groaned again.

"That's the spirit, big guy." Parker started pulling off fabric from the other side. "We'll have this sorted out in no time, bud."

The rested of us drifted away from the table as they got to work. "I'm going to take a look around," I said softly to Ivy.

Destruction and disruption. If that was all our saboteur was looking for, they were getting results. But was it their end game? Or a messy step on the path to a greater goal? How did sabotaging the play benefit anyone? My frustration was back in full force. A million questions and not nearly enough answers to go around.

"What are you up to, Howard Wallace?"

I jumped at the voice whispering over my shoulder. "Leyla," I said. "Keep sneaking around like that and we'll make you a permanent member of the team."

Leyla slid around to stand beside me, shoulder to shoulder as we surveyed the room together. "I'm a member of the press, Howard. I have no interest in joining your little gang." She smiled at me. "But I'd love to know why you're hanging out at rehearsal while your B-team's bumbling around downtown."

I clamped down on the horde of smart remarks that wanted to pop out. No sense in serving her a juicy sound bite for free. "I'm sure you would," I said.

"You're checking up on the—" Leyla made air quotes with her fingers "—accidents, right? This play couldn't be more cursed unless someone actually broke a leg."

I snorted at that and then schooled my face back into business mode. "Same terms as the graffiti case?" I pulled out the pack of Juicy from Ivy and popped a piece in my mouth.

Leyla shook her head, a greedy little glint in her eye. "We can share info, but I'm not sitting on anything," she said. "People love a good disaster."

"Guess I'll just have to be faster than you," I said.

Leyla hummed in amusement, snatching the pack out of my hands. "Five bucks says I can guess your shortlist." She took two pieces before handing it back.

"You're on," I said, snapping out a bubble.

She cast a sharp eye over the gym. "Mrs. Grantley-Smythe, our illustrious Parents' Association volunteer and—" Leyla tapped a finger on her chin, contemplating. "Parker 'Bow Down to Me' Bowman."

"Interesting."

"Who'd I miss?" she demanded.

"We're also keeping an eye on Mrs. Pamuk and Nina," I said, pointing at the eighth-grade stage manager.

"Oh, well, you're wrong about both of them so that's fine," Leyla said.

"I'm wrong." I turned back to Leyla. "How do you figure?"

"Mrs. Pamuk is doing everything she can to keep this show on track. The Parents' Association is insisting on meeting with her at least once a week," Leyla said, ticking off her facts. "It's their money boosting the show up this much, but their definition of donation is 'bought and in charge of.' They're questioning everything."

"And you know that because?"

"My mom's a member." Leyla shrugged. "Basically, anything goes wrong, the spotlight will fall squarely on Mrs. Pamuk. It's in her best interest to make sure everything goes right. Why do you think she's letting Parker help so much?"

"No clue, but I'm sure you're going to tell me."

Leyla's eyes gleamed as she grinned. "His mom's on the PA board. A happy Parker's a happy board."

I filed that intriguing tidbit away for closer examination. "What knocks Nina out of the running?" I nodded over at the short brunette standing by the stage. She held a notebook in a white-knuckle grip, face impassive as Parker lectured her about something.

"Nina goes to theater camp every summer," Leyla said. "This is her first time as stage manager. If it goes well, she'll get to stage manage at camp, which will help get her into the high school Drama Club which looks good on her transcript and so on."

I stared at Leyla as I processed her revelations. "*How* do you know all of this?"

"I am the eyes and ears of this school." Leyla waggled her fingers through the air. "Also, I socialize and talk to people. They tell me things. I have a trustworthy face."

"People need to get better at reading faces."

Leyla scowled at me. "She's also friends with Ellis so I hear things that way. We've hung out a few times."

Ellis Garcia was the head of the Grantleyville Middle School Drama Club and current co-lead of the play. We'd crossed paths over cases and were familiar with each other. On the borders of friendly. I glanced over to where she was on the stage, running through a song with her co-star and Mrs. Pamuk.

Leyla followed my line of sight and chuckled. "I'm surprised Bradley didn't make the list."

"Considered it," I said, frowning as the guy in question hit a rough patch of notes. Bradley Chen got tangled up in my first major case at school. He'd been in so deep it almost cost him his place in the Drama Club. "He wouldn't risk it," I said. "Not when he finally has a chance at the spotlight."

"What makes the other two tick for you?" Leyla cocked her head to the side, casting a curious eye to where Parker still labored over Audrey II while an agitated Scotty fluttered around him.

"They're the unknown elements," I said. "I find it hard to believe that Parker's here out of the goodness of his heart. He's working an angle alright, but I haven't figured out if it's the one we're looking for." I leaned back against the wall to cut a glance across the room where the actors were pacing out their moves. Blocking or something, Ivy had said. Mrs. Pamuk and Mrs. Grantley-Smythe had their heads bowed together over their notes.

"As for Mrs. Grantley-Smythe," I said. "Frankly, the fact that she's a Grantley was enough to put her on the list. We also suspect she's more 'voluntold' than volunteer. If she's used to the sports crowd, I can't see her being happy with this new assignment."

"Makes a certain kind of sense." Leyla held her hand out.

I stared at her upturned palm. "What?"

"You owe me five bucks," she said.

"You didn't guess everyone on the list," I pointed out.

"Because you had it wrong."

"They were still on the list."

Leyla grumbled at me. "Next time I'll account for your misinformation in my educated guesses."

"The angles, Leyla," I said. "Can't forget to look at all the angles."

....-.. .- ...   -   -... --- .-

The rest of rehearsal was a relative bust. Parker decided I was wandering too close to the set and roped me in to helping him and Scotty work on Audrey II.

I spent the last half hour up to my elbows in glue and chicken wire, listening to Parker recount his glory days as head of the GMS Drama Club. Reaching my limit, I'd made my excuses in order to duck out early. Checking in with Miles and Carl wasn't a lie—I did that on my way home and had no news to show for it.

Groaning, I flopped down on my bed face first.

"What's wrong, Howeird?"

I lifted up my head enough to see Eileen lounging in my doorway.

"Did they finally have enough of your 'help' at rehearsal?" She smirked. "Ivy send you home?"

"Your use of air quotes does not invalidate my efforts, Eileen." I scrambled up on the bed to glare at her.

"Ooh, you are grumpy." Her eyes widened as she laughed. "What's going on? Getting jealous of how cool and talented your friends are?"

I threw a pillow at her, and she caught it easily, squishing it between her hands. "Go away, Eileen," I said. "I'm working."

My sister took that as an invitation to wander in and pull up a seat in my desk chair. "This the case Ivy was talking about? With the play?"

"Yes," I grumbled. "We're treading water. I can't get any

leverage on our suspects, and in the meantime, our perp keeps running wild."

Eileen sat up in her chair. "You need dirt on people?"

"Facts would be good," I said. "But I'll start anywhere at this point."

"You obviously have not spent enough time in the theater," Eileen said, tossing the pillow at my head. "If you want the gossip, and I mean the good stuff, you need to go to the right people."

"And those people would be?" I prompted after her expectant pause.

My sister stood up and twirled her hands in the air before posing dramatically in the doorway. "The *actors.*"

She swanned out of my room, leaving me to stew.

Well. That was annoyingly helpful.

Parker Bowman might be an unknown quantity to me and Ivy, but there were people who'd been around during his heyday with the Drama Club.

And they were both starring in this year's play.

Chapter Nine

I showed up promptly in the gym for rehearsal on Wednesday afternoon. All other cases and meetings were shoved aside. I had an appointment to keep and I would not be sidetracked.

"Howard," a voice squeaked. "Howard, help." I whipped around to see Scotty struggling under the weight of his plant as he tried to move it across a table. Jogging over to lend a hand, I almost staggered as we hefted the great green beast over about two feet. Hard earned inches, every one.

"Thanks," Scotty panted out between breaths. "Thought I was going to drop her there for a second. That would have been a nightmare."

"Made a lot of progress since yesterday," I said, poking at a leaf.

"No touching," Scotty said as he slapped my hand away. He grinned sheepishly at me. "It took a ton of work to get back to this state. I might be a little overprotective."

"It looks good," I said. Making sure to keep my hands to myself, I leaned in for a closer look. "The vines are pretty realistic."

Scotty nodded as he took a step back to view his construction with a critical eye. "Needs bigger teeth though."

A clatter of feet running across the gym floor interrupted before I could question that statement. Ashi and Ivy hopped up to Scotty's station. I immediately straightened up. "What's happening? Did you see something?"

"No." Ivy sighed. "Our group member's out sick, and we need to practice our choreography. Ashi said Scotty's been practicing with her."

Ashi beamed at Scotty as she poked at the giant green fabric leaves on the table. "And he's really good," she said. Scotty blanched as he tried to subtly get between her and the plant.

"We were hoping he could run through the moves with us," Ivy explained.

Scotty blushed and moved Ashi's hand away from his

project. "I don't know," he said. "It's one thing helping you at your house, but here? In front of everyone?"

I held a finger up. "Who's supposed to help me keep an eye out if you three are all working on your moves?" I asked. "We're supposed to be working a case here."

"What's the point in saving a play we haven't practiced for, Howard?" Ivy said with a roll of her eyes. She and Ashi dragged Scotty away as he looked back at me, desperation filling his round face.

"Should I keep working on this then?" I pointed at the plant.

"Please don't," Scotty called back, more than a little panic creeping into his voice.

I had an appointment to keep anyway. Scanning the room, I spotted Ellis and Bradley warming up by the stage. I snaked my way through the various crews working on sets and props around the gym floor. Ellis looked up as I approached, finishing her lunge with a small smile of acknowledgment. Bradley scowled as he caught sight of me. He quickly moved into arm stretches, waving them around, keeping a convenient circle of personal space.

"Ellis," I said with a cordial nod. "Bradley. Tell me: how does it feel to have your fearless leader back in action?"

"Parker?" Bradley spat out before he managed to dial back his wrath. "It feels fine. Totally fine. Lovely to have the gang back together again. Nice to see Parker taking on a *behind-the-scenes* role."

Ellis flopped down on the wooden bench pushed up against the stage, stretching her legs out in front of her. She ran a hand over her close-cropped curls with a wry grin. "I agree with Bradley," she said. "It sucks."

"Now, why would you say such a thing, Ellis?" I copped a seat on the bench beside her, ducking out of the way of Bradley's still-whirling arms.

"No need to dance around, Howard," she said. "You've talked to him. You know why."

"Because he's an arrogant, narcissistic, patronizing over-actor who doesn't even go here," Bradley hissed.

"That was going to be my guess," I said. "Bradley beat me to it." I turned in my seat to face Ellis. "Why do you think he's here? Besides the welcoming committee," I said with backward nod at Bradley.

"Helping out, like he says." Ellis shrugged. "I understand it, really," she said. "All the years Parker was in Drama Club they had nothing. No budget, no attention. Did you know this is the first time the school is letting us have an evening performance?"

I shook my head.

"Parker put his heart and soul into this club," Ellis said. "We all do. Look at them." She swept out a hand to the room at large. "Everyone here is working themselves to the limit. Trying to pull something together. Something that when it works, it's magical." She took a slug from a bright blue water bottle, wiping her mouth on her sleeve. "We all put blood, sweat, and tears into these plays. Maximum effort for one fleeting moment." Ellis sighed into her chest before looking back at me. "It's always intense, but this year, it's different."

I itched to take out my notebook, but sat on my hands instead. Anything that broke the bubble we were in could stop up the stream of information coming my way. "How so?"

Bradley abandoned his pretense at stretching to gracefully collapse on Ellis's other side. "We have actual sets for one thing," he said. "And costumes. Money to make our own props. Kept the raiding of our own houses to a minimum this time around."

"It's the first time we've started to feel like we're putting on a real play," Ellis said. "I don't blame Parker for wanting to be a part of that."

"I do," Bradley said. "He had his turn. We're supposed to be in charge of the Drama Club, and he's taking over everything. Did you hear him talking to Mrs. Pamuk about changing our choreography? *Again?*"

Ellis patted Bradley's knee. "He might be assistant director, Bradley, but you're still the lead," she said. "No one's going to take that away from you."

"He's certainly not," Bradley said. "I've waited over two years for this. It's my time to shine."

"So, yes, Howard," Ellis said, ignoring Bradley's rambles. "He's here. He's irritating. But he's also helping to keep this production together when it seems to be falling apart at every opportunity so it's not like we can turn him away."

"Was there anything else?" Bradley rose up from the bench, jostling my legs as he went by. "Because we should finish our warm-up. We have a lot of new moves to learn."

"No, that answered my questions," I said, tipping my hat. "Thank you for your time." I ambled out of the way of Bradley's leg lifts and headed back down to the other end of the gym.

Digging my notebook out of my pocket, I scribbled down as much as I could. Money was pouring into the Drama Club for the first time. The siren song of a supersized production called Parker back to his home turf. How benevolent could his intentions be in the face of such ramped-up resources?

Stood to reason that Parker could be jealous he never had the chance to perform on this scale. Could see him taking a swipe at things for that reason alone.

The question was: how jealous did he have to be to take down a whole show?

My musings were interrupted as Ivy rushed up and ripped the notebook out of my grip.

"You've got to get downtown," she said breathlessly, her brown eyes filled with alarm.

I tied my coat, tension pulling my focus tight. "What happened?"

"Carl just texted me," she said. "Marvin's place got hit again."

Nearly out the door, I stumbled when Ivy's last words hit my retreating back.

"But they lost the guy."

Chapter Ten

Blue and I burned rubber all the way to downtown. I was going to owe her another trip to the shop after this. We skidded to a stop at the lot beside Marvin's, and I made quick work of locking my trusty ride up to the chain link fence. By the time I got through the shop's front door, a ruckus was in full swing. Shouts from Carl, Miles, and Marvin spilled out onto the street before I could set a foot inside.

"Okay, okay. Enough," I said, bellowing to be heard over the uproar. "Tell me what happened. One at a time."

"I'm not impressed, Howard." Marvin thumped a fist into the shop's counter and sent a cloud of dust into the air. "That's what's happening," he wheezed, pointing a bony finger at the lot of us. "I hired you and then you turned around and palmed it off on these two yahoos. I hire Howard Wallace, I expect the job to get done right. What am I paying you for? Snack time?"

Embarrassment burned in my gut at the reproach. Marvin had every right to lay into us. I had made him a promise, and we'd failed to deliver. I'd failed. Whatever mistake Miles and Carl made was on me. Came with the territory of being in charge. Now I had to make it right.

I faced Miles and Carl. "What went wrong?"

"We were waiting for the perp," Miles said. "Across the street like we planned. Carl went to go get a snack from Marvin's, and I was keeping watch."

"I was only gone a couple of minutes," Carl said.

"Nothing was happening here," Miles said. "Hardly even anyone on the street."

They were dancing around the point so much they were gonna need new shoes. "How'd things tip sideways?"

"I saw a guy come out of the hardware store," Miles said, rubbing at the back of his neck as he grimaced. "It *looked* like he had cans of spray paint, and I thought I should check it out."

"You left your post unattended." Not hard to put two and two together to get negligence.

"For maybe two seconds, Howard," Miles protested. "I was halfway there, and Carl was on his way back to the spot. Then he shouted and started running toward the alley."

"There was a kid," Carl said, kicking at the faded linoleum floor. His cheeks flushed as he stared hard at his shoes. "Painting the wall again. I chased after him, but he took off down the alley. He was superfast, Howard. I tried to follow for as long as I could . . ."

"But you lost him," I finished for him. "We set our trap, could have caught the perp, but you guys abandoned your stakeout. Do you at least have a description?"

"He was wearing a hoodie and a hat," Carl said. "Gray, I think. Shorter than me."

"Most kids are shorter than you, Carl. Not helpful," I said, scrubbing a hand over my face. This operation had entered train wreck territory, but it might still be salvageable. "Let's check out the scene."

We headed out to the alley where half of Marvin's face was currently dripping down the bright white of the freshly repainted wall, Miles and Carl trailing after me like chastised puppies. "Sloppy work," Marvin sniffed at the masterpiece. "Did a better job the first time. That's what you get when you rush."

"He went this way?" I pointed down the alley, and Carl jerked a nod in agreement. Picking my way through the trash and old crates, I walked down to the other end to take a look around. The alley opened out into a narrow lane lined with garbage bins. Plenty of escape routes for our perp to choose from. We'd have had better luck if the alley was a dead end.

I spun around. "Hey, Marv!"

"What," he called out, not taking his eyes off the half-finished portrait.

"Which one of these is yours?" I kicked at the closest garbage bin.

"The one on the right."

I crouched down to inspect the bottom of the bin. Luck was on our side today. "Guys, come here," I said. Miles and Carl jogged over and gave the bin a dubious squint. "Get on that side. We're going to move this to block off this exit."

"That sounds gross and unnecessary," Miles said.

"Wouldn't be necessary if you'd stuck around and caught our suspect. Now gimme a hand." The metal screeched in protest as we shoved the bin into place. It took some serious elbow grease and tricky maneuvering, but it did the job. The small margin of space remaining on either side wouldn't be enough for anyone to get through.

"You know there's bylaws against this sort of thing." Marvin's voice floated over from the other side of the bin.

I scrambled up the rust-coated and distressingly slimy back to peer down at him. "They give you a warning first?" I asked.

"Yeah."

"Let me know if you get a letter, and we'll sort it out," I said, shooting a stern look at my associates. "But we're not going to let it get that far."

I walked back around to the front of the building with Miles and Carl trailing behind. "You still got that paint, Marv?" I called out.

He grunted in the affirmative.

"You two," I pointed at Miles and Carl. "Are going to repaint the wall. Today."

Miles looked up to the sky and groaned. "Again? Seriously?"

"And tomorrow," I said through gritted teeth, "I'm taking point on this."

"What?" Miles's head snapped back down, his eyebrows slamming together as one. "It's our case. We're handling it."

"It's the agency's case," I said. "And handling what? You're unfocused. Running down random leads. Splitting up.

Laying a trap open and then leaving it vulnerable? Clearly you need supervision. We're going back to basics, and we're going to do this right. Any arguments from you, Carl?"

"Do what you need to, Howard," he said, softly. "But we're not going to let him get away again."

"Not if I can help it." I left them to their cleanup and rode back home. Leaving the two of them to run this case was no longer an option. Having a crew was one thing, but they still operated under my name. I had worked too hard to let them squander everything by letting people down. Nope.

Somehow, before tomorrow, I had to figure out how I was going to work two cases at once.

Chapter Eleven

Thursday morning started off with a bang as Ivy slammed my locker door shut, nearly taking my nose off in the process.

"Morning, partner," I said. "Appreciate the assist, but what's with the velocity?"

"The costumes are gone." Ivy's jaw trembled with barely contained rage. "All of them," she said. "Ashi and I went to go grab hers so she could work on it at lunch, and the racks were empty."

"Did you check—"

"Yes, Howard," Ivy snapped. "We looked everywhere they could be. Even the janitor's closet. They've vanished."

"What did Mrs. Pamuk say?"

"Not much." Ivy blinked back tears. "She was too busy trying to figure out what we're going to do."

Seeing my partner look so defeated was unacceptable. I patted my pockets looking for a tissue, coming up empty. I held out my arm to Ivy, jiggling the sleeve of my lucky coat. "Use this," I said. "It's absorbent."

A wet chuckle drifted up as she wiped her eyes. "This is bad, Howard. Really bad."

"It's bad," I said. "And it's a big move. A risky move."

Ivy mulled that over, taking a breath to calm down. "Everything else that's happened so far could be written off as a mistake or an accident," she said, nodding slowly, shifting into investigative mode. "No one's going to be able to gloss over this."

I bumped shoulders with her as we headed toward class.

"We can use this," I said, aiming for a reassuring smile. "Keep an eye out. See how everyone reacts."

"Rehearsals are going to be fun." She caught my grimace and raised an eyebrow. "What?"

"I'm supposed to be at Marvin's after school," I said. "Get the graffiti case sorted before he and Mrs. Hernandez have to cough up the dough for that security system."

Ivy pushed her way through the crowd with a little more force than necessary. "Let Carl and Miles handle it."

"Tried that," I said, jogging a bit to catch up with her. "They goofed it, remember?"

"I knew this was too many cases," Ivy said, pausing outside of homeroom to kick at the wall.

"No. Hey, no." I ducked down to catch her eye, waiting to speak until we were properly facing. "This case is important. Just as important as any other one. We'll figure out how to work them both. I promise."

"Yeah?" Ivy smiled.

"Yeah," I said. "I hate to say this, but I think we need to have a meeting with everyone."

Ivy nodded and pulled out her phone.

"At lunch," I said. "But not in the caf."

"The office?" Ivy glanced up for confirmation.

"Perfect."

Close enough anyway. We were gonna make this work.

....-.. .- ...   -   -... --- .-

As soon as the lunch bell rang, Ivy and I headed to the girls' bathroom at the west end of the school. Aside from being familiar space, it was usually relatively deserted at this time of day. The one closest to the caf was the lunchtime hot spot. We should have the place to ourselves.

Ivy and I burst through the door, stopping short at the sound of a flushing toilet.

Scotty emerged from one of the stalls, whistling. "What?" he said, catching us watching him make his way over to the sink. "Have you seen the boys' bathroom?"

"Actually, that's a good point," I said as Ivy laughed. "Good aim seems to be more of a goal than a skill over there."

She made a face.

"Exactly." I nodded. "I gotta remember to go before we leave."

Ashi tumbled in as Scotty finished drying his hands. Miles and Carl were hot on her heels.

"Have you seen this?" Ashi held up her phone for Ivy and me to scrutinize.

"*Wardrobe Malfunction*," I read out. "Is that—a blog post from Leyla? Already?"

"Yup." Ashi tugged her phone back so she could scroll down. "Here's the best part." Ashi cleared her throat. *"When reached for comment, Parker Bowman, student director of the play, expressed shock and dismay at the news. Bowman will be organizing a clothing drive to attempt to replace the costumes before opening night. Donations can be left at the Grantleyville Senior Center."*

Ashi slipped her phone into her pocket. "There's a whole list of what we're looking for so maybe it will be okay." Her face crumpled as she began to cry. "This is all my fault."

"What? Ashi, no." Ivy grabbed Ashi's hand as Scotty patted her gently on the shoulder.

"I'm in charge of costumes," Ashi sobbed. "I should've—"

"Should've what, kid?" I grabbed some paper towel and handed it over. "Known that the costumes were our perp's next target? Slept at the school to guard them?"

Ashi mumbled into the paper towel as she wiped at her face.

"What was that?" Ivy leaned in.

"I said," Ashi fussed. "Where are we going to find another dentist costume?"

"There's a dentist?" I said half to myself. "Why is there a dentist?"

"You really need to read the play, man," Carl said.

"Howard," Ivy said, gesturing at a still leaking Ashi. "Focus?"

"None of us could have guessed this would happen or been able to stop it." I leaned against the sink as Ashi began to level out. "All we can do now is figure out next steps."

The bathroom door swung open suddenly. We all froze

as Ellis and Leyla elbowed their way into the room. I shot a look at Miles and Carl. "A little security on the door would be nice."

"You guys are talking about the play, right?" Ellis stood planted in the middle of our group, arms crossed. "We want in."

I pointed at Leyla. "Pretty sure she's already in deep. Didn't you see the blog post?"

"First of all," Leyla said, waving away my hand. "Don't get snippy. I'm a reporter. Bringing things to the public is what I do." She boosted herself up on the sink. "Second of all, yes, it was a great article. Thank you for noticing."

I fought back the urge to roll my eyes as she continued.

"And lastly, you're welcome. People are sharing the post like crazy, and donations are already pouring in. You'll have new costumes in no time."

"Oh," Ashi said, her face brightening. "That is good news."

Ellis scowled. "Good news in the face of something that shouldn't have happened in the first place. What are you guys doing to fix this mess?"

"Ellis is very serious about her theater," Leyla stage-whispered from the sink.

"Serious or not," I said. "You can't just waltz into the middle of our case."

The door creaked open, and Carl leaned over to slam it shut. He sat with his broad shoulders against it for good measure.

"We know," Ellis said, dipping her chin in acknowledgment. "Leyla already filled me in on what she could. Your little fishing expedition yesterday makes a bit more sense now, Howard."

"Trying to stay under the radar while we put the pieces together, Ellis," I said. "More people involved might bring unwanted attention."

"We could probably use the help," Ivy muttered at me.

"The play is important to me," Ellis said. "I want to help, but I'm not coming empty handed. We're bringing something to the table."

Leyla flashed jazz hands at us. "Intel."

I shot a look at Ivy, and she nodded. We could work with this. "Okay," I said. "Let's talk." I grabbed a patch of floor and took a seat. Pulling my lunch out of my bag, I rummaged around until I found my apple. Everyone else followed suit, and we formed a loose circle on the ground.

"Oh, I forgot!" Ashi exclaimed. "I brought cookies. Snickerdoodle?" She offered the container to Ellis who smiled ruefully.

"Can't," Ellis said. "I'm allergic to cinnamon."

"Shoot, I'm sorry," Ashi said, thunking herself in the forehead. She passed the container to Scotty on her other side. "I forgot."

Ellis scratched at her freckled nose and shrugged. "I never do. Don't worry about it."

Once everyone settled, lunches in hand, I turned to Leyla. "So," I said, around a mouthful of apple. "What d'you got?"

"You're still trying to narrow down your suspect list, correct?"

Murmured agreements came from all around.

"I called for quotes today," Leyla said. "Mrs. Grantley-Smythe had no idea the costumes had been stolen. She was appalled. And very surprised." Leyla munched on her cookie. The rest of us suffered through the dramatic pause.

"Now," she said. "When I got in touch with Parker, he said 'Is this about the costumes?'"

Ashi gasped, much to Leyla's satisfaction.

"Yes, I know. So troubling," she said. "Naturally, I immediately questioned how he already knew about the situation. He said he overheard his drama teacher talking to Mrs. Pamuk about it and whether or not they could borrow some costumes."

"That could be the truth though," Miles pointed out.

"Yes," I agreed. "But it's still odd. Combine that with the fact that—"

"Parker is the worst and nobody likes him," Ivy cut in.

"It's worth taking a closer look at Parker and his story," I said. "I'll be at Marvin's after school, and the rest of you can cover rehearsal."

"By yourself?" Miles sat up straight. "What about me and Carl?"

"Take at least one of us for backup," Carl said.

"After what happened," I started, halting when Ivy sang "*second chances*" under her breath. I side-eyed my partner, and she stared back, scrunching up her nose.

"Fine," I said. "But we do need extra eyes at rehearsal. Ivy, Scotty, Ashi, and Ellis are too busy to keep watch the whole time. Carl, you go with Leyla. I'm trusting you to stay alert and stay on task. Miles, you'll be with me."

Carl nodded.

"Wait a minute," Miles said, coming up a beat behind.

"Meet me at the front doors at the end of the day," I said. "On time. We'll head downtown from there."

The bell rang, and everyone started packing up. "We'll meet up tomorrow morning for reports," I said as they filed out.

With any luck, I'd be solving at least one case today.

Chapter Twelve

"So," Miles said, jogging alongside Blue as we rolled downtown. "I'm the untrustworthy one?"

"Unreliable," I corrected. "Not entirely the same thing."

Miles threw his hands in the air. "I showed up every day. I sat through the boring stakeouts."

"You also ran off on a hunch and missed the actual perp," I said. "You keep making rash decisions like that and you'll never close a case."

"You seem to manage," he muttered.

Blue and I stopped short to pin him with twin glares. "Excuse me?"

"I'm sorry," Miles said. "But were you an awesome detective when you started? Was Ivy?"

"Ivy was actually pretty good from the get-go."

Shoving his hands in pockets, Miles kicked at the sidewalk. "Well, I'm still figuring it all out. And I'm never going to get better if you don't actually let me try."

"That's . . . not a bad point." I set my feet back on the pedals and continued down the sidewalk. "I'll try and walk you through things a little more."

Miles nodded, long legs keeping pace with me and Blue until we hit downtown. We stopped at Mrs. Hernandez's to lock up my ride. Leaving her at Marvin's would be a dead giveaway of our presence.

We were nearing Marvin's when a sound caught my ear. I put my arm out in front of Miles and motioned for him to listen. I heard it again—a faint hissing noise.

Like someone was using a can of spray paint.

Miles's eyes widened, and I held him back.

Slow, I mouthed. *Slow.*

We crept along the storefronts to the alley. When we were steps away, the front door of Marvin's shop opened up, and the man himself stepped out with impeccably horrible timing.

"Hey, Howard." He waved. "Other kid."

Two sounds hit me at once. The first was the shattering of

any hope we had of catching the suspect by surprise. The second was the rattle of a spray can hitting the ground, spurring me and Miles to burst into action. We tore around the corner in time to see our perp already on the move. A slight kid in jeans and a black hoodie was booking it down the pavement.

Miles and I followed in hot pursuit. Reaching out, I nearly had a hand on his sleeve when it zipped out of reach.

The kid climbed neatly up the dumpster and over the other side. Too neatly.

"Come on," Miles yelled, scrambling up the front. "We can still catch him." His hand slipped in something better left unexamined. "Give me a boost, Howard."

"No need," I said, bracing an arm against the wall to catch my breath. "I know who it is."

"How?" Miles hopped off, one hand held carefully off to the side. "You didn't see his face."

"I could tell when he climbed over the dumpster," I said, reviewing that practiced vault in my head. I'd seen it once before during a very memorably messy case.

Miles took a step back. "You could tell who it was just by how they climbed?" He raised an eyebrow at me.

"It's a very distinctive climb." I sighed.

....-.. .- ... - -... --- .-

"Toby Turner," I said, gesturing at the tidy blue house in front of us.

"That kid?" Miles exclaimed. "The one who was snatching purses and tried to help you reverse dognap Spartacus?"

"That would be him." Toby and I had become acquainted over a number of cases. He was one of the youngest members of Grantleyville's most preeminent family of petty criminals. That tidy blue house was the façade for a felonious empire. It was a white picket fence of corruption. A garden bed of lawlessness.

"Doesn't look like anyone's even home," Miles said.

Come to think of it, Toby had been off my radar for a while now. He hadn't cropped up in any of the usual stomping grounds. I'd been holding onto the hope that he'd mended his ways. Apparently, he'd just been brushing up on a new skill set.

"What should we do?" Miles was vibrating beside me, itching to take action. "Do we look around? Check for evidence? Call the cops?"

I pulled out a pack of Juicy and offered him a piece before taking one myself. "I was thinking," I said, sliding the pack back into my pocket. "That I'd go ring the doorbell." I poked two fingers in his direction. "Watch and learn. This is lesson one in your retraining."

I strode up the sidewalk as Miles sputtered behind me. After brushing off my coat and adjusting my hat, I reached out and pressed the bell once.

Toby answered immediately. I knew he'd be keeping a lookout.

"Howard Wallace," he said, eyeing me warily behind the safety of his crossed arms. He had the twitchy energy of someone ready to bolt at a moment's notice. The constant vigilance of the constantly delinquent.

"Toby." I smiled brightly and then sniffed. "I don't think you need to use quite that much turpentine."

"Oh, that's Grandpa." He leaned in to whisper. "Trying to get rid of his foot fungus."

"And I'm sure he appreciates you sharing that information. You missed a spot on of paint on your thumb, by the way."

Toby whipped his hands behind his back and glowered.

"We're here about your new hobby," I said. "I thought Ivy talked to you about making better choices."

He leaned against the door frame, a smirk creeping over his face. "I chose to be more creative."

"Might be creative, but graffiti's still a crime."

"I like to think it's the best of both worlds," Toby said. "Gotta keep a finger in every pie."

"Well, your artistic crime spree has the Business Association talking about putting up cameras downtown."

He paled at that news.

"I would think," I said. "Something like that would affect the extracurriculars of everyone in the Turner family."

Toby sighed, low and mournful. "What do I have to do?"

"Grovel," I said. "Lots and lots of groveling."

"Let me grab my coat." Toby headed back inside.

I turned to face Miles. "And that's how it's done. Detective lesson for the day."

Toby emerged, closing the door behind him. We headed back up the walk as Miles stood slack-jawed on the porch.

"I have no idea what I just learned," he said.

....-.. .- ... - -... --- .-

We herded Toby back to Marvin's place, practicing apologies along the way. Marvin was waiting out front, sharp eyes taking in our parade as we approached.

"Wondered where you disappeared to," he said. "This the guy?"

"This is the guy." I prodded Toby forward. "He has something to say."

"Hang on, hang on." Every joint in Marvin's body creaked and popped as he stood up. "I gotta call Alva. She needs to hear this, too." He ambled inside while we waited patiently on the stoop.

Toby blew out a breath and rocked back on his heels.

Most of us waited patiently.

"Hello," Mrs. Hernandez called out a few minutes later, hurrying up the street. "I brought coffee." She passed a cup over to Marvin as he met her on the stoop. "This is our rogue artist?" She peered owlishly at Toby over the rim of her cup. "Toby, isn't it? I keep hoping we'll meet under better circumstances."

"I admire your optimism, Mrs. H," I said, pulling Toby forward. "He would like to tell you and Marvin something."

Toby opened his mouth.

"Sincerely," I added. "With real emotion and possible tears."

He shot me a dirty look as I got shushed from all sides.

"Let the boy speak," Marvin said.

"I'm sorry," Toby said, clasping his fingers in front of his chest. "For painting without permission and vandalizing your place of business thereby possibly affecting your overall bottom line." He glanced over at me, and I gave him a short nod. Not quite what we practiced, but close enough.

"Now," I said, slapping my hands together. "Restitution.

Toby will be painting over all of his artwork as soon as possible. He will also be offering his services for any manual labor you may have up to say, twenty-five hours?"

Marvin squinted at Toby as he mulled over my proposition. "How long'll it take you to paint this over?"

"An hour." Toby shrugged.

"How long would it take you to paint it again?" Marvin asked. "But bigger?"

"Uhhh—" Toby looked between me and Marvin, and I returned his shrug. I had no clue where this was going.

"Bigger and with more colors," Marvin said, guiding our group around to the other side of the building. "No one can see it from that alley. Over here, we got the lot, southern exposure, and people get a clear view coming down the street. You do my face again, that was good, just make it bigger." He swept a hand through the air as he stared at the wall. "And then in nice, big letters, we put the name: Marvin's on Main. I like it. Be eye-catching. So how long?"

Toby's mouth opened and closed a few times before he shook himself. "Ten hours at least, depending on the weather. But I don't know about the paint—"

"Eh, yeah, yeah, never mind that," Marvin said, scratching at his chin. "I'll get you what you need. And you take the time you need to make it look good. Mrs. H might want something too depending on how mine turns out." Mrs. Hernandez nodded with a smile.

"What is happening?" Miles whispered.

"You went about it all wrong," Marvin pressed on. "You got talent, that's for sure. What you need is clearance because then, my friend—" he clapped Toby on the back "—you get paid."

Toby perked up. "I'm listening."

"We need to work on a business plan and a pay rate. Don't be afraid to charge a Grantley through the nose."

"What is *happening*?" Miles asked again.

"Marvin's creating a monster," I said.

"Tch, not creating, Howard," Marvin said. "Refining. Let's talk business cards, kid, starting with you not using this kid's as an example."

"I think we're done here," I said to Miles. "We'll send you our bill," I called out as we left Toby in Marvin's somewhat terrifying hands.

Finally, some progress.

One case closed meant we could turn our attention to the play. As Miles and I went to retrieve Blue, I wondered if Ivy and the gang had survived rehearsal. Fingers crossed they'd shared a bit of our good luck.

Chapter Thirteen

"It was a nightmare," Ivy said that Friday morning, thunking her head against her locker. "Parker gave us a lecture about 'responsibility' and 'being mindful of our resources.' Like someone forgetting to hang up a shirt was the reason all of the costumes were stolen."

"He was super rude about it," Ashi said. She handed me a chocolate chip muffin and passed one over to Ellis who accepted it with a grateful smile.

"The costume drive is going really well," Ellis added. "And he's taking all of the credit for that."

I glanced over at Carl who was being his usual silent self. "Did you catch anything?"

"I shadowed him the whole time," Carl said. "But didn't make much difference. He had an eye on me too."

"That could be a good thing." I turned it over in my brain. "He suspects we're watching him. If he's behind this, he knows why. Maybe with some pressure, he'll trip up."

"Or he'll get even sneakier," Scotty offered.

I shook my head, weighing the odds. "Someone who steals an entire play's worth of costumes isn't set on subtle. We've got the same ticking clock," I said. "He has a week to finish whatever he's got planned."

"Where does that leave us?" Ivy waved a hand at the group huddled around her locker.

"Help me get close to Parker," I said. "I can get him to crack."

Leyla caught me in a steady gaze. "Somebody's confident."

I cut her a grin. "I just bagged the Grantleyville Grafitti Bandit," I said. "This'll be a piece of cake."

....-.. .- ...   -   -... --- .-

With one week left to opening night, Friday's rehearsal was a zoo. Mrs. Grantley-Smythe was busy overseeing the revamping of the donated costumes. Mrs. Pamuk had her hands full getting the cast in shape for their musical numbers. And Parker was gleefully supervising everyone left over.

"You call this foliage menacing?" He held up a limp leaf to Scotty's face. "This is shoddy workmanship. Why did you change my leaf placement? It'll look like a trash heap on stage."

Scotty stammered, his face turning fire engine red. "Well, I—"

"Personally," I said, sidling in between the two of them. "I think a trash heap is the more menacing option."

"Howard." Parker turned to me. "Why exactly are you here?"

"You know," I said, steering him away from Scotty's table. "I've been meaning to ask you the same question."

Parker chuckled dryly, his easy smile not reaching his cold, assessing eyes. "I would think it's obvious," he said with a jerk of his chin to the hive of activity around us. "This production would fall apart without my help."

"Would it though?" I squinted at him. "Seems to me it's a pretty big group effort."

"Every group needs a leader," he shot back. "You know that as well as I do."

"I figured that'd be Ellis. She's the head of the Drama Club."

"Ellis is a talented kid," he said. "But it takes someone with experience to guide an operation of this scale." Parker leaned against the gym wall, fishing a small rectangle out of his back pocket. "Gum?" he offered.

I declined with a measure of grim satisfaction. I'd said it before, and I'll say it again—never trust a person who chews vanilla mint gum.

"Tell me something, Parker." I took up residence beside him on the wall. "Everyone talks about how great you were in the GMS shows." He preened a little at that. "The high school has a Drama Club," I continued. "Why are you spending your time behind the scenes here instead of on stage with them?"

Parker's jaw clenched as he stared ahead, but he quickly rallied, turning to face me. "You know what show the high school's putting on this year?"

I racked my brain trying to remember the title of the show Eileen had been gushing about.

"*The Music Man*," Parker spat out. "The same tired old show that hundreds of schools put on every year." He shook his head in disgust. "No, my skills are being put to much better use here. These kids need someone to guide them now that we have a budget to put on a *real* show."

We watched the rehearsal in silence for a few moments.

Ellis and Bradley had finally gotten in step and were nailing their number.

Parker shifted on the wall. "What about you, Howard?"

"What about me?" I kept my eyes on the show.

"We're pretty clear on my part," he said. "And your friends have all found their place. But aside from making the occasional mess, what's the point of you being here?"

I forced myself not to move back as Parker leaned in. "I'm here to support my friends," I said simply. "I go where I'm needed, and I do what has to be done."

Parker's expression changed with whiplash speed as he flashed his toothpaste commercial smile at me. "That's great, buddy. I'm glad to hear it." He clasped a hand to my shoulder and squeezed.

Tight.

"I'm going to talk to Mrs. Pamuk about what jobs we could have you do. Don't want to leave you at loose ends. Who knows what you'd get up to?"

He laughed and thumped me on the back before heading over to Mrs. Pamuk. Scotty crept up as soon as he left.

"That looked like it was weird and scary," he whispered. "Was it weird and scary?"

"I'm pretty sure Parker just threatened me," I said slowly.

Scotty frowned, adjusting a vine that was slipping out of place. "They why are you smiling?"

"Because we're getting to him," I said. "All we have to do is figure out where to apply the pressure."

Chapter Fourteen

I vy and I stood in the home office later that evening, putting the last of our updates on the case board.

"So Parker's definitely our lead suspect now?" Ivy flopped down on the ugly comfy chair.

"Yup," I said, moving his picture to the center of the board.

"That's good," Ivy sighed. "I actually kind of like Mrs. Grantley-Smythe."

I turned to raise an eyebrow at her, snorting at the thought of any Grantley being remotely palatable.

"I know, I know!" she said. "But you should have seen her working on the costumes. She was super intense, and, and, genuine about it. I've never seen anyone get so passionate about hidden zippers. I think she wants the play to work out as much as we do."

"Let's hope we can make that happen," I said as I stepped away from the board.

"What's your plan for tomorrow?" Ivy stretched out on the chair, feet kicking over one arm.

"Find a big stick," I said. "Poke Parker with it."

"Solid plan," Ivy laughed.

It was the only plan at the moment. We had to focus on Parker. Zero in on what made him tick. Getting inside his brain was key to figuring out his next move. The threads of this scheme were so tangled up, I couldn't figure out which end to tug on first.

"We should head in," I said, glancing at the clock. "Eileen'll flip her lid if we're late for dinner."

My folks were out for date night and Eileen was "babysitting." She'd conned my parents into the job—both for the money and to prove she could be trusted to take on bigger and better gigs. So far, she'd been surprisingly pleasant. I suspected there'd be a survey at the end of the night.

"Right on time for pizza," Eileen called out as we came in the backdoor and toed our shoes off on the rug. "Howard, can you grab the salad and take it to the table?" She smacked me with an oven mitt as I poked at the bowl in question. "Wash your hands! Don't stick your fingers in there. Everyone's going to eat it." Eileen held onto the bowl as Ivy and I washed up, arms curled protectively to ward off any germy fingers from her carefully chopped tomatoes.

I held out my hands for inspection. "Better." She plopped the bowl in my hands. "And Ivy, the juice from the fridge?"

We carried out our duties with the speed of two hungry souls as Eileen dished up the pizza. The three of us sat around the table to dig in.

"Now," Eileen said, before blowing on her slice. "How was school today, kids?"

I scoffed as Ivy giggled into her juice.

"I'm serious," Eileen protested. "That was a real question. Tell me about rehearsal."

"Ugh," Ivy groaned.

"That bad?" My sister's eyes widened as she chewed.

"The play's fine," Ivy said. "Disasters aside, I really like my part, but working with Parker is the worst."

"Parker?"

"He's a high school volunteer," I supplied. "Acting as student director."

"Ugh, Howard. You're disgusting. Chew, swallow, then

speak. It's the natural order of things." Eileen's forehead wrinkled as the pieces clicked together. "Hang on. Parker Bowman? Whoa. Good luck with that."

I exchanged a look with Ivy across the table. "Do you know him?"

"He was in Drama Club for a hot second," Eileen said. "It was an entertaining second at least."

Propping an elbow up on the table, I cupped my hand under my chin. "He said he left the group because he wasn't impressed with their choice of play. Being involved with our show was a better use of his abilities."

Eileen choked on her salad. "Yeah, no," she said as she coughed. "He threw a massive fit because he wasn't cast as the lead. Like a freshman can walk in and play Harold Hill. He might have been great at GMS, but he's up against a lot of talent at the high school." Eileen shrugged. "He was pretty insulted about being cast in the chorus so he quit. Loudly." She pointed her fork at me. "Elbows off the table."

I looked over at my partner whose mouth was hanging wide open.

"Howard." She grinned.

I nodded in awe. "That's a pretty big stick."

Chapter Fifteen

Ivy and I walked into the senior center on Saturday full of secret knowledge and the urge to wield it.

Ashi caught us at the door, her grim face stopping us in our tracks.

"New blog post," was all she said before thrusting her phone into my hand.

"*Empty Shop of Horrors*," I read aloud. Ivy and I skimmed through Leyla's latest. She highlighted sluggish ticket sales and questioned if the show would break even.

"I know they say no PR is bad PR," Ashi said mournfully. "But it doesn't feel like it."

"Leyla here?"

Ashi nodded as I pressed her phone back into her hand.

She and Ivy followed as I strode into the auditorium. Leyla was on a bench in the corner, painting her nails to match the vibrant blue of her bangs.

"Before you start yelling," she said as we approached. "Remember that none of it was a lie. Ticket sales were sad. The Drama Club is a small group. We can't rely on friends and family alone."

"You think making it sound like the play's going to tank will sell tickets?" Ivy put her hands on her hips as she stared down at Leyla.

"I know it will," Leyla said. "I had to capitalize on the costume story. People love drama, and we needed to keep their attention." She swooshed her fingers through the air before inspecting her handiwork. "This is a sportscentric town. Takes a little extra oomph to get people to come out for a show."

"That's your logic, but is it working?" I asked.

"Of course it is," Leyla said with a smug grin. "Ten more sales already this morning. And my blog has twenty new sub-scribers." Her eyes gleamed as she finished off her last nail with a flourish.

I didn't like her methods, but it was hard to argue against the results. I beat back the nagging voice at the back of my brain. More attention on the play might make it more difficult for us to operate, but Parker had to work under the same scrutiny. I could deal with road blocks as long as they were equal opportunity road blocks.

"Can everyone gather round please?" Parker's voice drew our attention to the front of the room. "Up here, up here, take a seat," he said.

Ivy and I kept to the back, angling for the best view for whatever was about to play out.

"Many of you have seen the news about our ticket sales," Parker began, taking a moment to glare at Leyla. "I know you're worried about whether people are going to come see the show. And you should be." He continued on over the swell of confused mutterings. "I was in this club for years, and I worked my butt off every day. Mediocre is not going to cut it. People don't show up for amateurs. They come out for stars."

Ellis stepped out from the crowd, moving to stand beside Parker. "That's a little harsh, don't you think? Everyone's trying their best here."

"Are they?" He pointed at Bradley. "Your co-lead over there messed up his solo seven times yesterday."

Bradley sputtered, a red flush spreading steadily down his neck. "That's why we have rehearsal," he said. "To get better."

"Better's not the goal, Bradley," Parker said. "Outstanding. Incredible. That's what you should be aiming for." He crossed his arms across his chest, staring a hard line down his nose. "That's why I'll be working one-on-one with you today. I'm not passing my legacy off to a hack who sings off-key."

Bradley's carefully blank reaction proved he was a better actor than I'd ever thought he was.

"Sorry I'm late, kids!" Mrs. Grantley-Smythe sailed into the room, garment bags slung over each arm. "Last minute stitching!"

"And that's how we're going to make this show great, guys!" Parker pumped a fist into the air. "Oh, hey, Mrs. Grantley-Smythe. How'd the alterations go?"

"Wonderful, wonderful," she said, setting her bags out on a table. "Less than a week until opening night, who's excited?"

Everyone clapped half-heartedly.

"Let's get this rehearsal going," she cheered.

Kids dragged themselves out of the huddle to spread out across the room. Scotty made a beeline for his plant project. Miles and Carl were with the tech crew going over sound cues while Ellis and Ashi gathered the other actors to run through blocking. Parker grabbed Bradley's elbow, dragging him from the group over to a corner, lecture already in full swing.

"That's going to be a problem," Ivy murmured.

I agreed. Hard to hound Parker when he'd made it his mission to hound Bradley.

"Howard," Mrs. Grantley-Smythe walked up to us with a flip of her perfectly coifed blonde hair. "Parker mentioned you could use a job," she said, her sing-song tone putting my teeth on edge. "I have some programs that need to be folded, and they have your name on 'em!"

"Sounds great, count me in," I said, grimacing over my shoulder at my partner. Ivy shrugged helplessly as she got pulled away to practice her number.

This was going to be trickier than I thought.

....-.. .- ... - -... --- .-

Not tricky.

Impossible.

Rehearsal had come to a close, and I hadn't managed to get close to Parker at all. He'd spent the whole time with Bradley, running lines and songs, sometimes adding Ellis into the mix. Not that I'd have been able to get to him without the Bradley buffer. Every time I'd turned around, there was Mrs. Grantley-Smythe with another "fun" job for me. Parker shot little smirks at me every time he caught my eye. I had been well and truly played.

By the end of the day, the show was in better shape, but our case was running in circles.

Ivy and I stood outside the senior center with the rest of the crew to debrief.

"Parker was intense today." Miles scrubbed a hand over his face.

"And weirdly obsessed with Bradley," Scotty said.

"He's escalating," I said, chewing a piece of Juicy and offering the pack around. "He managed to run interference on me without lifting a finger. He's going to pull something soon, but I have no idea what."

Leyla's face twitched as she cut her gaze to the ground.

"Leyla," I pressed. "Did you see something? What do you know?"

"I may have overheard Parker talking to Bradley about needing extra practice. They're going to meet up early on Monday," she said.

"At the school?"

"Parker said Mrs. Pamuk had cleared it because some staff will already be there and Pete can unlock the gym for them."

I ground the toe of my shoe into the sidewalk contemplating that development. Parker's frustrations and a closed rehearsal didn't add up to anything good for Bradley.

"What are you thinking, partner?" Ivy poked at my leg with her foot.

"We've got to be at that meeting."

"All of us, you mean," Miles said, motioning at the group.

Leyla rolled her eyes. "You don't think that would be a little conspicuous?"

"Only me and Ivy." I held up a hand before the protests could start. "We don't want anything to happen to Bradley, but we can't afford to tip off Parker either. This is our best bet."

I ignored the grumbles as we headed home. If I was going to beat Parker, I had to play it smart and use our best people.

And I was going to beat Parker. No matter what.

Chapter Sixteen

Sunday passed by in a blur of homework and procrastinated chores. I was itching for Monday morning to roll around, the desire to do something leaving me restless down to my bones.

Luckily, I had dinner at Ivy's house to distract me.

Maybe lucky was the wrong word.

Ivy opened the front door before I had a chance to knock. "Don't look so concerned," she said. "Mom's not even here yet."

"Oh." I perked up as I stepped inside.

"Is that Howard?" Lillian called out.

"Yes, Grandma."

I kicked off my shoes, and Ivy hauled me toward the kitchen before they even hit the ground.

"What can I do?" I asked as Ivy and I grabbed our aprons. We fell into the easy rhythm that came from months of cooking together. Lillian was determined to make us masters of the kitchen before we left home. When I pointed out that was a solid six plus years away, she'd sighed. Barely enough time apparently.

Veggies were chopped in short order, and chicken was sizzling in the pan when Mr. Mason poked his head in the door. "Any word from Bianca?"

Ivy's shoulders tightened as Lillian shook her head.

"She must be running late," he said, ruffling Ivy's hair before ducking back out.

Twenty minutes later, dinner was ready, and Mrs. Mason still had not arrived. Ivy and I set the table, taking great pains not to watch the clock.

"We'll keep it warm in the oven for a bit," Mr. Mason said.

By six-thirty, Mrs. Mason was nowhere in sight, and Lillian had had enough. We were startled out of our awkward silence by the slap of her hands on the counter.

"I'm starving," she said, pulling dishes out of the oven. "And I'm not letting this beautiful meal go to waste." She directed us on what to take, and we brought everything out to the table.

There was a brief, awkward pause when we all sat down. It was tight for space with the elephant in the room. Ivy stared resolutely at her plate, and Mr. Mason kept opening his mouth to speak and then closing it. I snuck glances at my partner, trying to gauge her mood. Cracking a joke to lighten the mood felt wrong. Talking about cases seemed trivial.

Lillian dove in once again to get things moving. She smiled and started dishing out the chicken. "Dig in, everybody," she said. "Hector, didn't the kids do a lovely job on those spices?"

Mr. Mason hummed appreciatively around a mouthful of chicken.

"Howard." Lillian turned to me. "Ivy said you caught someone doodling all over town. I want to hear about that. Spill."

I launched into the tale, and little by little, we all relaxed enough to enjoy the company. Halfway through the meal, Mr. Mason's phone buzzed. Conversation paused while he pulled it out to check the screen.

The line between his brows deepened as he frowned. "It seems your mother can't make it at all tonight. I'm sorry, Ivy."

Lillian's eyes narrowed as she pressed her lips shut, and Ivy leveled a flat glare at her father.

"I kind of figured that already," she said. "How many more of these does she get to miss before we stop trying to make it a thing?"

"Ivy." Mr. Mason spoke with the air of someone trying to keep a grip on their patience as it squelched through their fingers. "We've talked about this. Even though your mother and I aren't together, it's important that we still try to do some things as a family. There are going to be bumps as we figure it all out."

"I just had a very nice dinner with my family," Ivy said, waving a hand at the table. "The ones who cared about being here. And now, I would like to be excused."

Lillian and Mr. Mason let us make our escape. I expected Ivy was in for the rest of the argument after I left. In the meantime, we grabbed some cookies and headed up to her room.

"Ugh," Ivy threw herself on her bed, cookies held high to keep them safe. "I don't know if it's better or worse when she doesn't show up."

I patted her on the knee as I walked by. "Does it happen a lot?" I commandeered the desk chair and rolled it over to the bed. Ivy kicked at my feet when I attempted to put them on the bed.

"Eh, fifty-fifty," she said. "I don't know why she moved back here. This whole thing is beyond weird."

"How are you doing with," I waved a cookie in the air, "all of that?"

"Honestly?" Ivy propped herself up on her elbows. "Confused 'cause I don't really get what they think is going to happen with this exercise. Mad as heck when she doesn't show up. I don't know. It's pretty much a mess."

I'd only been to a few dinners, and I knew Ivy was understating that fact. I wished there was a way I could pull her out of the middle of it all. "A mess I can help with?"

She flopped back down on her back. "I will let you know."

We munched on our cookies in silence for a while.

"I've been thinking about tomorrow." Ivy sat up on the bed suddenly, brushing away crumbs.

"Thinking what?"

"We should bring more backup," she said.

I wasn't going back down this road. "No way," I said, shaking my head.

My partner's face set in a stubborn frown. "What's the point in having a team if we're not going to use them?"

"We use 'em plenty." I spun my chair around in a slow, lazy circle. "Not every job requires every one of us."

"You don't think we could use an extra set of hands? Carl and Miles have been dying to get in on bigger cases." Ivy grabbed the arm rests to stop my next rotation. "They're never going to learn unless they do more."

"You saw what happened when they got a bigger case," I said, looking her dead in the eye. "We'll give them other opportunities, but this is not the case to practice on. There are too many moving parts. If we're going to catch Parker in the act, we need smarts and stealth. Experience. One wrong move and he's in the wind."

We had enough balls in the air, and I was doing my best to juggle them. There were too many unknown elements at play. If we put part of this case in someone else's hands, that was one variable too many. We couldn't risk someone with less experience fumbling things.

There was a reason our names came first. We got the job done.

"The play is what's on the line here," I said. "Do you want to trust that in the hands of anyone but you and me?"

Ivy chewed at her lip. "Okay," she said. "Fine. I trust you."

"Good," I said. "I trust me too."

I kept laughing even as the pillow hit my face.

Chapter Seventeen

Monday morning, Ivy and I crept up to the school, keeping an eye out for our quarry as we stuck to the shadows.

My partner was humming away behind me.

"Ivy," I whispered. "What are you doing?"

"Working on our new sneak theme music. You like it?"

"I'd like it if it was quieter," I said. "Preferably silent."

Ivy huffed. "How do you want to do this anyway? Side door start?"

"Side door start," I agreed. "Puts us to the left of the gym and out of the sight line for the office." Last thing we needed was Mrs. Rodriguez, our principal, catching us sneaking into the school. She knew us well enough by now to harbor a general level of suspicion at any of our activities. Out of sight, out of mind was the best way to play it safe. "Then we can sneak in through the backstage and keep an eye out from there," I said.

She nodded, in tune with my plan. "How are we going to see around the set?"

Good question. I could always count on Ivy to help me see all the angles. The backdrop was already in place on the stage—a series of boards and screens put together to create the little shop. Finishing touches were being put on so it still rested at the front of the stage, held in place with a few well-wedged door jambs and a chair. Not something I was in any hurry to try and move.

"If we had more people—"

I cut off Ivy's line of thought with a shake of my head. We were too far along to bring anyone in at this point, and I stood by my decision. We couldn't afford to make the wrong play. The best person—the best people—for this job were me and Ivy. Parker's game came to an end today. Ivy deserved a chance to enjoy her time in the play in peace. I was going to make sure of it.

Wallace and Mason Investigations was on the case, and we always came out on top.

"If we stick to the sides with the curtains, we should be

able to peek through," I said, shooting her a confident grin. "Let's go."

We walked casually over to the side door. Quickly, but not at a pace to arouse suspicion. Once inside, we zipped down the hall, ducking past open doorways. Annoyingly, Ivy's sneak music was already stuck in my head. She grinned at me like she knew it, too.

We slipped through the door leading to the backstage. I kept an ear tuned as we silently climbed the steps in the dark. We avoided the creaky stairs, carefully lifting our feet, barely allowing ourselves to breathe. Our exceptional stealth skills aside, it was quiet.

Too quiet.

Bradley and Parker should have been rehearsing by now. Or one of them should have been there waiting for the other. But the gym was silent with half the lights still turned off. Ivy and I made our way onto the stage. I blinked as my eyes adjusted to the semidarkness.

"That's not good," I said, keeping my voice low.

"What?" Ivy whispered.

"Well, first of all, I can see the gym," I said. "Through the set."

Ivy blinked in shock as she stepped forward to take a

closer look. The canvas was sliced through on its frames. It hung in tattered strips forming jagged windows for us to peek through.

"Do you think he hit anything else?" Ivy gasped. "The costumes."

I wouldn't put it past Parker to try and strike on as many fronts as he could in one fell swoop. Divide our attention and resources. It'd be a smart move. It's what I would do. "You should go check on them," I said to Ivy.

"They're in the Drama Club classroom," she said. "Mrs. Pamuk started keeping them there after what happened."

"Go," I said. "We need to know if anything else has been damaged."

Ivy hesitated. "I don't want to leave you here alone."

"I'll be fine." I waved her off. "I want to poke around and see how bad the damage is. Come back when you're done, and we'll try to figure out where Parker and Bradley have gone."

"I'll be back in two minutes," Ivy promised before dashing back down the stairs.

I had plenty of work to do until then.

Squeezing around the set, I stepped to the front of the stage. I crouched down to take a closer look at the damage and let out a low whistle. Paint swathed the front of the set in long, angry red slashes. Parker took his sabotage seriously. This was a bang-up job.

Assuming it was Parker. There was no sign of him anywhere. No trace to pin this mess back on him. The gym might be silent and still, but there was a thrumming undercurrent of tension almost pulsating in my chest. It felt like I was being watched.

The door to the gym slammed open with a bang, and Bradley stormed into the room. "Okay, Parker, I'm here," he said. "Let's get this over with."

He caught sight of me standing motionless on the stage, and his jaw dropped. "Howard?"

Oh.

Of course.

How did I not see this coming? How did I miss it? I was an idiot. Bradley wasn't Parker's target. He wasn't setting him up. That would've been too easy.

No.

Parker was setting *me* up.

"What did you do?" Bradley gasped as he ran over to the stage. "What did you *do*?"

"This is not what it looks like," I said.

Bradley shook his head, walking up the stage steps to take in the carnage.

"Okay, it's half what it looks like," I amended. "But it's definitely not what you think."

"I think Parker was right." Bradley whirled around to face me.

Wait. "What?"

"He told me to watch you. Said you've been hanging around because all of your friends are in the play, but you're jealous. Mad that they don't have any time for you."

I shook my head, trying to figure out how to counteract Parker's massive spin job.

"I mean," Bradley scoffed. "You already tried to wreck the set once. Makes sense you came back to finish the job."

"You've got the wrong end of the stick here, Bradley," I said when a flash of color backstage caught my eye. Maybe Ivy was back. She could help me make Bradley see some sense. I heard a faint scraping sound. The backdrop began to wobble.

Not Ivy then.

"We have to go," I said to Bradley, looking down to see the door jambs shifted out of place.

"No." He shoved me back with both hands. "We're staying

here until Mrs. Pamuk comes and you can tell her what you've done."

The backdrop creaked. "Parker's back there messing with the set, and I haven't done anything but try to help you," I said prodding Bradley to move backward.

"Parker's not even here. Stop lying. And stop trying to leave. I'm not letting you get away with this." He grabbed my arms as the backdrop began to topple forward.

"Look out," I cried, pushing him back, trying to launch us both out of the way.

Bradley lost his footing and with his hands gripped tight around my sleeves, we both fell off the front of the stage.

Chapter Eighteen

The crash was deafening. As the set toppled forward and slid down to the floor, Bradley and I flew through the air. Our momentum carried us far enough out of the way to avoid getting pinned, but the landing was far from graceful.

Scotty's plant broke our fall.

And then our fall broke Scotty's plant and the table it lived on. Bits of green paper and fabric floated through the air as the dust settled. Once I could get air back in my lungs, I took stock. Ears ringing, but nothing seemed more than bruised. My landing could have been worse. It felt surprisingly squishy.

"Get off of me," Bradley grunted. "You idiot." I rolled to the side, and Bradley struggled to get up. He instantly flopped back down with a moan. "My leg," he groaned. "I think you broke it."

"I didn't break anything," I said, pulling myself out of the wreckage. "You would have been fine if you moved when I said to."

"This is all your fault." Bradley lay starfished on the ground. "You ruin everything."

"Statistically impossible." I held out a hand. "Can you walk?"

"What part of you broke my leg do you not understand?"

"The part where you're not a doctor," I said. "I was asking to see if we could move you somewhere more comfortable before I go get help. Lying on chicken wire can't be good for you."

Bradley groaned. "Leave me here to die."

Actors.

The door opened and Mrs. Pamuk rushed in. "What was that noi—what happened?" She ran over to Bradley to help him sit up.

"Howard destroyed the set, and then he attacked me."

"None of that is true," I said quickly.

"Are you calling me a liar?" Bradley started forward before falling back with a pained cry. "I saw what I saw."

"What you think you saw and what you actually saw are not the same thing." Bradley scowled, and I pressed on before he could keep twisting the situation. "The set was like this when I got here, and I only pushed Bradley when it started to collapse. I didn't want it to fall on us, but then we fell off the stage."

Mrs. Pamuk pursed her lips, clearly full of more questions. "First things first, let's get Bradley to the nurse's office. Are you okay, Howard? Did you get hurt?"

"Bumped and bruised," I said, helping her haul Bradley up from the other side. "I'll be fine."

We managed to get Bradley out into the hall with minimal whimpering. I caught a glimpse of Ivy peeking around the corner and jerked my head at her. Better to steer clear of this mess. She was out of sight before Mrs. Pamuk looked up.

"The play. What about the play?" Bradley was wailing as Mrs. Pamuk made soothing noises. It was a good question though. With one move, Parker had taken out a main prop, the set, and a lead. The better question was why.

"Why?" Mrs. Pamuk asked.

I blinked and focused back on her. She passed Bradley off to the nurse and stood in front of me with a concerned frown. "Why would you do that, Howard? What happened?"

Dread began to build in the pit of my stomach. Talking my way out of this was beginning to look less and less like an option. "I told you I didn't do it."

"But why were you even in the gym?" She pressed a hand to her forehead. "What are you doing here so early?"

"I was coming to see Ms. Kowalski," I said. "To talk to her about an extra credit assignment for English."

A plausible lie. She'd taken points off my last project for arguing my way out of my original objective. "I heard a noise in the gym when I walked by. Seemed weird, and I thought I should check it out," I continued. "I found the set like that when I went in, and then Bradley came by and you know the rest."

"I really don't think I do," she murmured.

I shrugged, trying to project an air of innocence.

"Well, come on," she said. "We need to go explain all of this to Mrs. Rodriguez."

....-.. .- ... - -... --- .-

Four hours later, I was getting into the car with my parents, slapped with a week's suspension.

The talk with Mrs. Rodriguez had not gone well.

No one was buying my extra credit story. A person with a file as thick as mine wasn't often given the benefit of the doubt. My previous incident with set design was also getting laid out as some kind of malicious act. Like I would never volunteer to help out a friend. Clearly, I needed to work on my PR after this mess was sorted out.

With my back against the wall, I had no choice but to come clean. I laid out my suspicions about the play without mentioning Parker. I didn't have enough proof yet to name names. Mrs. Rodriguez was pretty steamed to hear I was investigating on school property again. The kicker came when we got the call about Bradley.

He had a hairline fracture.

He was out of the play.

I was out of luck.

Without enough proof in my favor, I was kicked to the curb until next week. Parker now had free reign over the play and no one to stop him.

My parents got into the front seat, and Pops started up the car.

"Now before you say anything, let me talk." I leaned forward as far as my seat belt would go, spitting the words out to get ahead of any protests. "This is not my fault," I said. "This was a setup. A frame job. I'm the patsy here. The sacrificial goat—"

"Howard." Pops cut me off with a wave. "Calm down. We believe you."

I gaped at them. None of my planned arguments covered that outcome. I was at a loss, left grasping at the next easiest response. "What."

"Give us a little credit for knowing our kid," Ma reached back to pat the hand that gripped the top of her head rest. "You're capable of a lot of things, Howard, but deliberately hurting someone is not one of them."

"Accidentally harming them, we can totally see," Pops added. "Which means we need to have a chat about exactly what kind of mess you've gotten yourself into."

He pulled into the driveway, and we headed into the house. Ma and I sat at the kitchen table while Pops grabbed us all a drink.

"So," he said, taking a seat. "Someone's been messing with the play, and you've been looking into it."

I nodded, tracing a finger through the condensation gathering on my glass.

"You want to give us a name so we can help you out?" Ma prompted.

"I can't," I said for what felt like the hundredth time that day. "I don't have enough evidence. It's my word against theirs." I looked up to meet my parents' stares. "That's not a game I do well at," I said. "Bradley's word is what got me the week's vacation."

"I think breaking the rules helped with that," Ma said sternly. "If you have nothing else to share, then we should talk about your punishment."

I knew this was coming.

"No phone," Ma said.

I couldn't remember the last time I actually had phone privileges so that wasn't much of a sacrifice.

"No internet," Pops said. "And no Ivy."

"What? No Ivy?" Whatever happened to the punishment fitting the crime? This was cruel and unusual.

"We'll see how the next few days go and maybe you can earn back some friendship privileges."

"Listen, Howard," Ma said. "We believe that you believe there's something going on. And if you give us a name, something to work with, we'll talk to the school. Try to help work things out."

"And if not?"

Pops shrugged. "You've got a week to think about it. Or find better clues."

"Frank!" Ma exclaimed, slapping a hand on the table.

"Once you're not grounded," Pops said quickly. "And not on school property. Follow the rules."

Ma sat back, pinching the bridge of her nose.

"Now go to your room," Pops finished up. "Think about what you've done."

I trudged up the stairs, a muffled sigh of "Really, Frank?" floating up behind me.

Think about what I'd done. Been doing that all day. I closed the door to my room and collapsed on my bed. The events of the case played over and over as I racked my brain trying to figure out where I went wrong. Every step. Every word. Every question. Doubts clouded every move. How did Parker get the upper hand? More importantly, how was I going to solve this case while I was stuck at home, cut off from Ivy and the crew? Without my help, they'd fall apart.

We were sunk.

Chapter Nineteen

Twenty-six hours.

Twenty-six hours, forty-three minutes, and fifty-two seconds since the start of my solitary confinement. Denied all contact with the outside world. No indication of when I'd see the sun once again. No hint at freedom on the horizon.

A shuffling noise outside had me sitting up in bed. The door to my cell flung open and the weak hallway light outlined a dark silhouette. Apparently, isolation was not punishment enough.

"Why are you sitting in the dark?" Eileen stomped into my room and ripped open the curtains. I recoiled into my sheets, shielding my eyes from the streams of light bursting through the window. "I thought only Ivy joined the Drama Club."

"The instructions were to think about what I've done," I said. "This is how I reflect. In silence. Among the shadows."

Eileen snorted. "Your brood is running dangerously close to a pout. Maybe this will cheer you up," she said, tossing a bag onto the bed beside me.

Any offer of help from my sister generally had strings attached. I eyed the bag warily. Inconvenient, sometimes painful strings. "What's that?"

"All of this suspicion and Parker still pulled one over on you," Eileen said, shaking her head. "I hope you're taking this time to brush up on your skills."

Grabbing the bag, I yanked it open and peered inside. And blinked. And looked again. "It's a phone," I said. "Where'd you get a phone?"

"You have friends in low places, little man."

"Carl." I patted the phone affectionately.

"Well? Don't let their delinquent efforts go to waste. Turn it on." Eileen shook her head as she walked out the door.

Powering up the phone, I endured a multitude of beeps as the notifications flashed over the screen. Texts from everyone with condolences and updates on the situation at school.

Scrolling through the messages, I mulled over the barrage

of information. The set was still a mess. Rumors were running wild about what exactly happened to it and Bradley and my role in things. According to Ivy, rehearsal was a nightmare. Tensions were high. Blame was being tossed around. And Parker was in the middle of it, cool as a cucumber.

My stomach clenched at the thought of him, lording his victory over everyone, while I was grounded, attempting to stay in the loop through secondhand reports. How did things spiral so quickly out of my control? How could I be expected to solve anything with my hands so thoroughly tied?

I threw the phone back down on the bed. "This is a disaster," I groaned. "I can't believe I'm stuck here. Parker's going to get away with everything."

"What are you talking about?" Eileen poked her head back into my room.

"The play. This case. I'm out of the game. My hands are tied," I said. "I can't investigate. Can't find the clues we need. I'm not there to gather the evidence, to stop whatever it is Parker has planned."

Eileen steepled her fingers and pressed them against her mouth, thinking as she walked over to my bed. "I'm hearing a lot of 'I' statements from you," she said, taking a seat beside me. "Here's one from me. I think you're a dummy."

I shot her a glare and huffed out a breath. "How is that helpful?"

"You know who's not a dummy?" Eileen waggled her eyebrows at me. "Ivy. And if the rest of those kids made it onto your team, they're probably okay too."

"They're still learning," I grumbled.

"Then give them instructions." Eileen tapped the phone against my forehead. "You trust Ivy," she said, and I nodded. "Let her take point, and the two of you should be able to get the rest of your team in shape."

She tossed the phone into my lap, and I turned it over in my hands.

"You know why a play is successful, Howard?"

I flopped back on my bed. "You're going to talk to me about teamwork, aren't you?"

"No," she said. "Your team is fine. You're the problem."

Burying my face in my sleeve, I groaned. "Because I'm a useless detective who can't even investigate his own case."

"Who's in charge of a play?" Eileen pulled my arm away to catch my eye. "The director," she said, not waiting for me to guess. At least this lecture wouldn't require my participation. "But the director can only do one thing to make sure the play is a success."

She stared at me expectantly. Guess it was interactive after all. "What do they do, Eileen?"

"They know that they're only as good as the people they work with. One person can't take on every role, but a smart director finds the right person for every role. And gives them the space to do their job." Eileen tapped a finger on my nose. "A play is only great when everyone feels like they're a part of it."

"Point made," I said, batting her hand away. "I screwed up. Knowing that isn't helping me fix it."

"The Howard I know doesn't give up this easily," Eileen said. "He's usually annoyingly persistent." She patted me on the head. "I know I was born with all of the charm, but I thought I left you at least a little smarts. Enough to beat a punk like Parker anyway."

I let out a small smile at that. "He's managed to trip me up so far," I said sobering up quickly as I looked over at my sister.

"He's one guy," Eileen said. "One mildly talented, very rude, hugely egotistical guy. What do you always say? 'Work with what you've got?'" She punched me in the arm as she stood up. "If you think about it, you know you've got a lot more to work with."

Eileen headed out the door. "I'll distract Mom and Dad

for a bit," she said over her shoulder. "Talk to your crew, Howard."

"Eileen?" I called after her.

"Hm?"

"Thanks for this." I waved the phone at her. "And the talk."

"No problem," she said, a fierce smile stretching across her face. "Happy to help. Nobody messes with theater. Not on my watch."

She shut the door, leaving me to contemplate my next move. I texted Ivy to ask how we could organize a meeting.

A few minutes later a group chat cropped up.

ME Hi, guys.

ASHI 👏 👏 👏

ME I should start by saying I'm sorry. You guys were right. I should've brought more backup. I underestimated the situation.

MILES I'm screenshotting this.

CARL K

IVY Apology accepted.

SCOTTY MY PLANT.

ME I'm sorry about that too. Although, it was mostly Bradley's fault. He's the one who tripped.

LEYLA Can I quote you on that?

ME Leyla, no. This is all off the record.

ELLIS Nice apologies. Great discussion. But what about THE PLAY? We need a set, a giant plant. Oh. And A NEW LEAD BY FRIDAY.

ME I have a plan for the first two. I know a guy.

ELLIS: ????? Share.

ME: You guys know him too. Miles, can you talk to Toby?

MILES: Graffiti kid? You want me to go talk to him? At his house? By myself?

CARL: I'll go with.

ME: He's got the speed and skills we need to fix the set.

SCOTTY: And Audrey II.

ME: ?

SCOTTY: That's the name of the plant you destroyed, Howard!

ME: And Audrey II.

MILES: You think he'll actually help?

ME: I think you can find a way to convince him. Talk to Mrs. Pamuk about giving him community service hours. I'm sure he needs them. Give him the right incentive, he'll help fix everything.

MILES: I'll try.

ELLIS: YOU WILL DO IT.

MILES: I will talk to him tonight.

IVY: What are we going to do about Parker?

ME: I don't know. I wish I could be there tomorrow.

IVY: I might have an idea about that.

ASHI: 😍 👍

We went back and forth for a few more minutes while Ivy laid out her plan. It was a pretty good plan. Possibly our only opportunity to figure out Parker's endgame. If everyone did their part, it could actually work. I left the chat feeling the first spark of hope in two days.

Maybe I couldn't do this, but we could.

Chapter Twenty

The next morning, I sat on my bed, scrolling through Leyla's latest blog post. It was a doozy.

A Star Reborn was the title. I skimmed over the details of the Bradley incident. No need to relive that. But I paused over an interesting bit. Apparently, the school and the Parents' Association held an emergency meeting about the state of the play last night. It was open to concerned parents, and a large crowd showed up. Everyone agreed things were not good. They were worried how the play could continue with no set and no co-star. Mrs. Pamuk was quoted as assuring everyone that the set situation was under control.

Well done, Miles and Toby.

My jaw dropped when I saw their solution for Bradley's replacement.

Parker.

Always there to lend a hand, always knows best, Parker.

"There it is," I breathed out. The missing piece clicked into place. This was his endgame all along. If he couldn't be the star in high school, he could reclaim the GMS spotlight. Wormed his way in, made himself indispensable, and then swooped in to save the day. The little weasel.

Leyla noted a few protests from some of the parents over a non-GMS student taking on such a large role, but with no one else prepared to take the part and so little time before opening night, there was no other choice if they wanted the show to go on.

"Knock, knock." Pops poked his head in the door as I shoved the phone under my pillow. "How's it going in here?"

"As expected," I said, scooting over to perch on the end of my bed. "Serving my time, reflecting on my misdeeds. Digging my escape hole."

"Good stuff," Pops said. "I picked up your homework from school. There's an extra credit assignment in there from Ms. Kowalski." He dropped a stack of books and papers on my desk.

"Extra what?" I scowled.

"That's the thing about a cover story, Howard." His eyes twinkled with laughter. "Sometimes people believe it." Pops winked as I groaned, closing the door on his way out.

I poked at the pile with a grimace. There were a few hours to kill before rehearsal. I had no way to work on the case until then. A distraction wasn't the worst thing. Maybe something mindless would help me take a step back—get a clearer picture of things. Sighing to myself, I picked up the first page.

....-.. .- ... - -... --- .-

Pacing my room, I stared at the phone in my hands. "Sometime today, Scotty," I muttered. Rehearsal was starting any minute and not being there was almost physically painful. Like a pull in my gut, tugging me toward the school, smacking me against the invisible barrier of my grounding. Ivy's plan was good, but the lack of action on my end was a tough pill to swallow.

The video call finally came through, and I smacked the accept button. Scotty's round face filled the screen.

"Hi, Howard," he whispered. "You ready?"

I nodded. "Yeah, let's go."

Scotty slipped the phone into the front pocket of his

shirt, camera facing out. I had a clear view of the gym, and the sound was only slightly muffled.

We'd settled on Scotty as the best bet for this mission. He was part of the play so no one would question his presence, but, as backstage crew, he had more freedom to move around. I could do without the narration though.

"Ah, yes," he said to himself. "And here we have my plant, Audrey II, on her way to being restored to her former glory." Scotty walked up to his worktable where Toby was hard at work reshaping the papier-mâché around the chicken wire. "A little rounder at the top there, Toby. I had a perfect curve before."

Toby stopped his movements and pointed a paste-covered finger at Scotty. "You want to finish this up? I got about a billion other jobs to get done, and I could do without the backseat crafting."

"No, no," Scotty said. "You're doing a wonderful job. I'll help soon." The camera tilted as Scotty leaned in to pat a piece of green fabric. "I'm so happy she's in such good hands. Audrey II had been through quite a bit over the last few weeks. At this point, she's more Audrey Four. Maybe Audrey Five. I don't know if you heard—"

The flat look Toby leveled at Scotty had his mouth

clicking shut. "Right, yup, leaving you to it. Looking great, Audrey II!"

The camera jerked forward, and Ivy came into view, tugging Scotty toward the front of the room.

"Hurry, Scotty," she said, glancing at his pocket. "Mrs. Pamuk is talking. *Everybody* should hear this."

Scotty settled off to the side, and I had a solid view of Mrs. Pamuk standing in front of the stage. Parker and Ellis flanked her on either side.

"It's been a rough go," Mrs. Pamuk said. "And I appreciate everyone's hard work. We're not giving up. Friday is opening night, and we need to focus on that." She looked around the room solemnly. "I know what happened to Bradley was a shock," she said. "But we still have our star—"

Parker smiled.

"—Ellis," Mrs. Pamuk continued. "And luckily, Parker has agreed to fill Bradley's shoes. Chins up, deep breaths, let's get this show on the road."

Parker's smile crumbled at her words. That couldn't be good. His eyes narrowed as his hands fisted at his sides.

Mrs. Pamuk might've just widened the target on Ellis's back.

Ever the professional, Parker recovered with lightning

speed, clapping his hands together. "Okay, guys," he said. "You know your assignments. I want lots of energy and focus today. No phones. No yammering. We have a lot of work to do."

The crowd broke up, and Scotty headed back to his work table.

"Scotty." Parker's voice drifted through the speaker. "I thought I said no phones."

Scotty turned, and Parker's smug mug came into view.

"I heard," Scotty said. "Don't worry, it's off. I'm hard at work over here. Recreating my masterpiece."

I ran a hand over my face, careful not to make a sound.

"Mm-hm, may I see it?" Parker held out his hand.

"My phone? Why?"

"Hand it over, Scotty," Parker said, voice hard as steel.

My view spun a few times as Scotty handed over the phone. We'd set the call up without video on my end and my number was unlisted in Scotty's phone.

Still. I held my breath as Parker looked at the screen. His icy blue eyes filled up the small window, a spiteful light flickering in their depths.

"Are you enjoying the show, Howard?" He spoke softly. Gently. His calm tone one of a pleasant chat between friends. "Did you like my present?"

Parker's words were almost drowned out by the thud of my heartbeat.

"I hope you're appreciating it more than Bradley." He brought the phone up to his nose. "Stay off my stage," he hissed.

The screen went black.

My mind began to race as the phone fell out of my hands onto the bed. How did he know I was there? How could he have figured out our plan? Why was he always one step ahead?

I choked on air, coughing as I realized the only possible answer.

We had a *mole*.

Chapter Twenty-One

A mole.

A leak.

Our very own stool pigeon passing around secrets like a fresh pack of Juicy. Hot spikes of betrayal burned in my gut as I sat down heavily in my desk chair. Someone from our crew told Parker I'd be watching rehearsal today. I couldn't believe it. Didn't want to. This was my team, my friends. The thought that one of them would rat us out made me ill.

But the facts were there, staring me in the face. Parker couldn't have found out about our plan unless someone told him. Sensitive intel being passed along right under my nose. And for how long? My heart sank as the pieces started to fall into place with dizzying speed.

This wasn't the first plan Parker ruined. The Bradley debacle dropped into sharp relief in my brain. Of course Parker knew Ivy and I would be at the gym on Monday morning. Someone helped him set that trap. Helped him put Bradley out of commission. He kept getting the jump on me because someone was giving him a leg up. But who?

I buried my face in my hands with a groan. One step toward solving this case had sent us a flying leap back. I grabbed my notebook from the desk and wrote out the names of each member of the crew.

Me. Ivy. Miles. Carl. Scotty. Ashi.

Chewing on my pen, I stared at the list before adding Leyla and Ellis. They'd been helping with the case as well and knew as much about it as the rest of us.

I crossed out my name with a firm stroke.

There. Progress.

Ivy's name was next. If there was one thing I knew for sure it was that my partner had no hand in this. I'd bet the agency on it. I'd bet Blue on it. She had my back as firmly as I had hers.

Circling the six names left, I sighed and thunked my head down on the desk.

Why would anyone from our team help Parker? What did they have to gain?

That was the frustrating thing about a motive—it only had to make sense to the person wielding it. At this point, the who was a more pressing issue than the why. Ferreting out our blabbermouth would help stop Parker before he did any more damage.

The phone started buzzing on my bed, and I scooted over in the desk chair, rolling along the floor. A quick peek at the screen showed messages from Ivy.

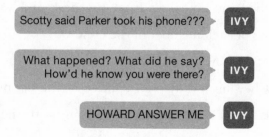

Scotty said Parker took his phone??? **IVY**

What happened? What did he say?
How'd he know you were there? **IVY**

HOWARD ANSWER ME **IVY**

Questions with answers that needed more than a text message response. We had to put our heads together in person to figure this mess out.

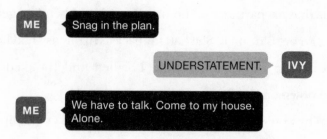

ME Snag in the plan.

UNDERSTATEMENT. **IVY**

ME We have to talk. Come to my house.
Alone.

IVY: What about your house arrest? I thought you weren't allowed to see anyone?

ME: I'll take care of it. Meet me at the fence by the driveway at 7. Don't let anyone see you.

ME: Stick to the shadows.

IVY: ...

IVY: You really need to get out of your house.

ME: Just be there.

IVY: I will.

IVY: IN THE SHADOWS.

My partner: the comedian.

Tucking the phone under my pillow, I returned to the list. A little over twenty-four hours until opening night. Fingers crossed that was enough time to find a rat and catch a snake.

....-.. .- ... -   -... --- .-

"Howard! Dinner!" Eileen's voice rocketed up the stairs, punching through my focus. I startled out of my chair and swept the case notes into a drawer. Best not to leave out any evidence that I was working a job during my sentence.

"Do you want to eat? Come on!" Eileen hollered. After a quick final inspection that nothing incriminating remained, I hurried down to the kitchen.

"Plates," Pops said with a nod at the cupboard without looking up from the sauce he was stirring. I pulled down a stack and brought them over to the table.

"Hi, sweetie," Ma said, pressing a kiss into my head as she walked by. "How was your day?"

"Law abiding." I took a seat when Pops brought over the pasta.

"That's new and exciting for you," Eileen said. She smirked at me from across the table. "Wonder how all your minions are getting along without you. Think they got the play up and running yet?"

"Guess we'll find out tomorrow," I said.

Pops froze halfway down to his chair, glancing over at Ma as she set down her glass.

"Howard," she said, eyeing me carefully. "You're suspended."

"I am aware of that." I tried to figure out where this was going as my folks exchanged another glance.

"That means you can't go to the play, Howard," Pops said. "You can't go to the school full stop. That includes extracurriculars."

Right. I should have figured that. Made perfect sense. "I'm sure Eileen will be happy to reenact it for me," I said, shrugging it off. "And Ivy said they were going to be recording it in case I wanted to see it done in tune."

Eileen kicked me under the table. "Ha ha, dweeb."

I let the rest of the dinner conversation flow around me. Missing Ivy's Drama Club debut stung, more than I expected it to, but it was the least of my worries at the moment. Keeping an eye on the clock, I plowed through my plate. The hour hand sluggishly hit seven o'clock as we finished tidying the kitchen.

"Gonna take out the garbage," I said as I closed up the dishwasher.

Ma's head whipped up at that. "What?" She put the last of the leftovers in the fridge and took a step back to cast a suspicious eye over me. "Why?"

"Because it's my job?" I tugged the bag out of the bin, tying the top tightly.

"And since when do you do this job without me having to chase you down and hound you about it every week?" Hands on her hips, Ma stood in the doorway, blocking my easy exit outside.

"My time in solitary changed me," I said. "No more shirking my responsibilities."

Ma didn't look convinced, but she let me pass. I scooted out the door, bag in hand, attempting to project an air of respectability and calm as I went by. Ma's eyes narrowed. That woman could read intentions from a mile away. "This is a five-minute job, Howard," she said. "I'll be timing you."

The door shut behind me as I headed out onto the drive. Ivy's head popped up instantly from behind the fence separating our driveway from Mrs. Peterson's. "I'm here," she called out in a harsh whisper.

"Stay out of sight," I said. "I'll meet you there." Grabbing the garbage and recycling bins by the handle, I hauled them down to the end of the driveway. The rattle of the wheels against the pavement made enough of a racket to cover the sounds of Ivy moving through the bushes.

Mostly.

I set the bins on the curb as Ivy emerged from the foliage beside the fence, scowling and grumbling while brushing bits of leaves off her arms. "Stay there," I said, waving her back with a slight flick of my wrist. "Don't want anyone to be able to spot you from the house."

Ivy sighed but took a step back. "No one'll spot me, Howard," she said. "I wore my stealth clothes." She gestured at her outfit with a flourish and a wide grin. Her head-to-toe black getup was stealthy alright—if you ignored the fact that her shirt read SNACK ATTACK and had a hot pink cupcake brandishing a sword right smack in the middle.

"Did you buy them special?"

"Ignore him, he's jealous." Ivy patted at the cupcake. "Besides," she said, waggling her fingers through the air. "I'm in the shadows. Practically invisible. Now tell me what's going on."

"We have a mole." I cut to the chase, not wanting to waste my precious time on the outside. "Somebody from the crew is feeding Parker intel on the case."

"Who?" Ivy gasped. I shot her a look as I lifted the lid on the recycling bin.

"That's what we need to find out," I said. I sifted through the bin, picking out boxes to break down in case Ma looked out the window to see what was taking so long.

"I guess asking them is out of the question." Ivy scuffed the toe of her shoe along the ground, forehead creased as she worked through our options.

"Someone's already lying to us," I said. "We ask, they all say it's not them, how do we know who's telling the truth?" I wanted to believe every single one of them, but the evidence was plain and clear. There was no denying the fact that almost everyone on the team had lied in the past. I couldn't take their word at face value.

The porch light came on, and Ma stuck her head out the front door. "Almost done there, Howard?" Ivy ducked back behind the fence as I waved a plastic bottle at Ma.

"Soon," I said. "Just sorting through this stuff. Someone keeps bagging the recyclables. And by someone, I mean Pops."

Ma gave me a long look before chuckling. "Okay," she said. "I'll tell him. Hurry up, and come back inside."

"Will do." I waited for the door to shut before turning back to my partner. "The direct approach is going to get us nowhere," I said. "We're not going to figure out who our snitch is unless we smoke them out."

"Like set a trap?" Ivy crossed her arms against her chest, wrinkling her nose at the idea.

"It's the only way," I said. "Parker's going to keep using them to get what he wants. Stop the mole, we stop Parker."

"He's already got the lead," Ivy said. "What more does he want?"

"I don't think anything will be enough for Parker. That's what makes him dangerous." I slapped the lid back on the recycling bin. "But we can use it against him too."

"But we don't know who the mole is," Ivy said.

"Easy," I said. "Six possible moles—we lay six traps."

"Howard," Ivy said, rubbing her hands over her face, frustration coloring every drawn-out syllable. "You're stuck at home, I'm clearly on my own. How could this possibly work? What are we using as bait?"

I smiled at Ivy through the fading light, and she stepped closer to the fence as the streetlights came on one by one. "Oh, I'm going to hate this plan, aren't I?"

"The bait," I said, stealing her flourish move from earlier, "is me."

"Yup. I hate it."

Chapter Twenty-Two

I t was all fairly simple as far as intricate and complicated plans went. There was no time to work on the nonexistent plan B so this was our do or die. If this failed, our mole would never be unmasked, leaving the future of the agency on shaky ground. Impossible to keep a team together when you don't know who to trust. And failure meant Parker would be free to carry out whatever remained of his underhanded schemes.

Not on my watch.

Friday morning, I sat on my bed and believed this plan would work. Considering I was still under house arrest, it was one of the few contributions I could make. Everything else fell on Ivy's shoulders.

After hashing out the details, I got to work immediately after she'd left last night. A simple text, sent individually to each member of the team.

> **ME**
> Found out new information about Parker from Eileen. Meeting Ivy in the regular spot to check things out. Radio silence. Steer clear. Don't want anyone else involved in case we get caught.

The key to every message was listing a different time for my meeting with Ivy. My partner would wait in the girls' bathroom at each appointed time. Finding out I was sticking my nose into things was enough to spur Parker into action last time. Hopefully it would offer the same draw this time around. Sending Ivy in on her own felt like a risk, but we had no other choice.

Stuck in my room, I was desperate to be in the thick of it, right there with Ivy in the middle of the action. What if she missed a vital clue? What if having another set of eyes and ears around caught the one thing we needed to crack the case? What if Parker struck out again and made Ivy his target?

I couldn't think like that. This was the best plan for the situation at hand, and I had to trust Ivy to carry it through. The only thing I could do in the meantime was wait.

....-.. .- ...   -   -... --- .-

Ivy sat on the back of a toilet in the girls' bathroom, staring at me glumly through the screen of her phone. "This is getting old," she said. "What if we're wrong? What if no one's the mole and Parker found out about things in some other completely random way?"

"The odds of that are incredibly low," I said. "We've only gone through half of the crew. At least we've narrowed the field." The hour before school had been a complete bust. Ivy hung out in the bathroom, waiting for someone to show up, waiting for anything suspicious to happen, but no dice. Miles, Carl, and Ashi actually followed instructions to stay away. I was more than a little shocked. And relieved none of them proved to be our resident weasel. But we still had three more to go.

The creak of the door cut through the silence in the bathroom.

"Shh," Ivy said. "Someone's coming." The screen went dark as she slipped the phone into her pocket. Footsteps walked across the bathroom floor, faintly echoing through the empty room. A jiggling noise as someone tried to open the door of Ivy's stall.

"Occupied," she said.

"Ivy?" Mrs. Rodriguez called back. Jackpot.

There was shuffling as Ivy opened the door and came out of the stall. "All yours," she said.

"Sorry," Mrs. Rodriguez said. "I didn't see your feet."

"Oh," Ivy said. "Sometimes I put them up . . . for leverage?"

I slapped a hand over my mouth to muffle the groan.

"Is the teacher's bathroom not working?" Ivy asked.

"It's fine," Mrs. Rodriguez said. "I like to make the rounds at lunch and check up on things. But I'm glad you're here. How's Howard doing?"

"Howard?" The scratchy slide of fabric filled the speaker as Ivy shifted in place. "He's fine," she said. "Home. Grounded. I haven't heard much from him."

Silence. I leaned in, willing someone to talk so I could get a sense of what was going on.

"I'm glad he's taking the consequences of his actions seriously," Mrs. Rodriguez said finally. "It wouldn't do for him to make things worse by violating the terms of his suspension. Something like coming to the school when he's not supposed to. That would be a very bad idea."

"Nope. Yup. He's at home. No worries about that. Oh, look at that. Forgot to wash my hands." The rest of Ivy's ramblings were drowned out by the water hitting the sink and then the crunchy creaking turn of the paper towel dispenser.

"Yup. See you later, Mrs. Rodriguez," Ivy yelled. After a few fumbles, the screen cleared, and my partner's face came back on the screen. "She's gone," Ivy said. "She checked all the stalls while she was talking to me. You think—"

"Someone tipped her off?" I said. "Definitely. Do you remember who had the beginning of lunch time slot?"

Ivy frowned. "Yes."

I shook my head. "Looks like we found our mole." And things were about to get messy.

....-.. .- ... - -... --- .-

Closing my eyes against the scene streaking past the phone screen, I listened as Ivy ran through the cafeteria. Now that we'd identified the mole, my partner was doing her level best to track them down.

"Spotted," Ivy wheezed into the phone. "Leaving the caf. In pursuit."

Now I watched the floor tiles whiz by as she chased down our answers. I didn't want to miss any of the action. Especially if Ivy ran into trouble. Stopping abruptly, my partner raised the phone to her face and held her finger to her lips.

Headed into the Drama Club room. Going to sneak up.

Ivy held the phone up so I could see as she peeked around the doorway.

"I did what you said. I don't know what more you want." Leyla paced back and forth between the tables, her back to the door as she blew out a frustrated breath. "The time wasn't wrong," she said. "That's what he sent me. He probably got caught trying to leave his house."

Leyla paused as she listened. "I don't think that's necessary. I got what I needed. You have the lead. It's done."

She straightened up suddenly. Ivy inched further around the doorframe and I found myself peering into the phone for a closer look.

"What does she have to do with it?" Leyla said. "It's not like you can play every role, Parker." She threw a hand in the air. "Relax, no one's here to hear anything. Tell me more—"

"Park—"

"Okay, but—"

"No, you don't—"

"Listen—"

"You *can't*—"

"Don't hang up—*Parker!*" Leyla tossed her phone down on a table and scrubbed her hands over her face, letting out a muffled scream. She stood like that for a moment before sniffing and wiping at her eyes. She reached for her phone again, and my view flipped as Ivy spun back out into the hall.

Ivy's hand was pressed up against the screen, but the speaker was left clear. "Oh, hey, Leyla." My partner's voice came through loud and clear.

"Ivy," Leyla said, back to her usual cool and composed self. "What are you doing here?"

"Looking for Mrs. Pamuk," Ivy said. "I had some questions about tonight."

"Check the staff room."

No one spoke. I sat on the edge of my bed, curling a fist into my forehead, waiting. For Ivy to ask a question or give me the all clear. Or for Leyla to confess everything. Any sign that something was happening, and they weren't just standing there staring at each other.

Ivy's voice broke through first. "Was that all?"

They *were* standing there staring at each other.

"Is Howard coming to the show?" Leyla asked. Where was she going with this? Leyla wasn't one for idle chitchat. I hunched closer to the phone, hoping to parse out the meaning behind her words.

"He's suspended," Ivy said.

Another beat of silence.

"That doesn't answer my question," Leyla said.

Quiet rustling came through. Ivy nodding? Shrugging? I hated not being there for this.

"Parker's coming early," Leyla blurted out. "To set up."

Interesting.

"Okay," Ivy said slowly. "Good to know."

Rapid footsteps faded away, and Ivy's face came back on the screen, eyes wide. "Did you hear all of that?"

"Yup." I nodded. "Why would she tell us Parker's going in early? Another trap?"

"If it is," Ivy said, glancing down the hall after Leyla, "she didn't sound too happy about it. Whatever she has going on with Parker doesn't sound like that much of a partnership."

"Maybe that didn't come from Parker," I said, replaying the whole conversation in my head. "Maybe that was just for us."

"Think Leyla was trying to give us an edge?" Ivy frowned. "Why?"

"Not sure," I said. If it was a setup, Leyla would've been a lot smoother, but I could be wrong. Lying to your friends was weight anyone would crumble under eventually. But something told me there wasn't much Leyla did by accident. "Gut feeling. In any case, we can't know for sure so we can't trust it. Proceed with extreme caution."

"None of your training covered how to do that."

I rolled my eyes at Ivy's smirk. "You're hilarious, but I mean it. Parker's unpredictable so we need to be smart."

"Okay," Ivy said. "What's our next move?"

"We get the team," I said. "And we stop Parker for good this time."

Chapter Twenty-Three

Stopping Parker required me actually leaving the house. I wasn't about to let that be the final bump to trip us up. Come five o'clock, I was busting out that front door—with or without permission.

Preferably with.

Distracting myself with paperwork, I finished the last of my assignments from school. Extra credit English assignment included. I took a solid minute to feel smug about that before turning my attention to the case. Ivy had arranged for the crew, minus Leyla, to meet us at the school. We'd break the news about Leyla's betrayal to them then. No use getting them all worked up and possibly jumping the gun.

I drummed my fingers over my desk as I watched the

clock in my room. Using all of my willpower, I urged the seconds to move forward. Finally, with an agonizingly slow speed that even Blue could admire, the numbers clicked over to five o' clock. It was go time.

I sidled into the kitchen where Pops stood, sipping tea and scrolling through his phone.

"Heeeey, Pops," I said.

"You can't leave."

I held a hand over my heart and staggered back. "You don't even know what I was going to say."

"You took an unprompted shower, did a full sidle in here, and had about three too many *e*'s in that 'hey.'" He side-eyed me over the screen. "You trying to tell me you weren't angling to leave?"

"Okay, yes, I was," I said, rolling back on my heels. "But for a very good reason. I need to go see Ivy."

"You're grounded."

"You said I might be able to get some time off for good behavior."

Pops set his phone down and sighed. "Why do you want to go see Ivy?"

"To wish her luck before the play—"

"It's break a leg," Pops said automatically.

I leveled a flat look at him and recognition dawned.

"Oh, right," he said. "Too soon."

"It's her first big event in Grantleyville," I said. "She's had a lot on her plate. You know what she's been dealing with. I want to give her some support. She's been on her own all week, stressing about the play and everything that's going on with her mom. She needs a friend right now. Just for a little bit. Please, Dad?"

He stared at me before heaving out a breath. "Okay," Pops said, resolve crumbling. "But listen: there are strict ground rules here. Your mother and I are taking Eileen to the play so I am trusting you to go and come straight back here. Promptly. No detours. We will know if you don't. Understood?"

"Yes, sir." I tore out the door and headed to Ivy's on foot. I couldn't risk taking Blue and having her spotted at the school.

A familiar car was parked in the drive as I walked up to Ivy's.

"We have a problem," my partner said as she opened the door. "My mom's here."

Ivy tugged me inside, and I spotted Mrs. Mason arguing in the kitchen with Ivy's dad. Lillian stood off to the side, watching with a silent frown.

"She just showed up," Ivy said. "She wants to take me out to dinner before the show. I said I couldn't and—" She gestured at the scene in the kitchen helplessly. Mrs. Mason was ricocheting around the tight quarters of the kitchen, arms crossed tight while she paced. Ivy's dad leaned against the counter, gripping the top as he stood firm against the storm. Angry words spilled over the threshold to land at our feet.

We drifted over to the doorway to listen in.

"I'm allowed to spend time with my daughter," Mrs. Mason said.

"And we agreed there should be a schedule," Mr. Mason shot back.

"Like our Sunday dinner you decided to skip this week." Ivy stepped into the room.

"And I'm sorry about that, sweetie. Something came up." Mrs. Mason smiled. "Right now, the adults are talking, okay?"

"Yeah, about me," Ivy retorted. "Maybe I would like to have a say in my schedule."

"Ivy, honey—"

"No, Dad," Ivy said, shaking as she got the words out. "I don't think we should have to go along with whatever she wants. Our stuff's important too. She can't pop in and out and expect us to go with it."

"Ivy, that's enough," her mom said, but Lillian cut her off with a wave.

"No, Ivy is right," Lillian said. "She's worked hard on this show. If she's made plans with her friends, we should respect that." She shot a look at Mrs. Mason. "It's important to follow through on these things."

"Well, if you don't want to spend time with me." Mrs. Mason sniffed.

"Not what I said." Ivy sighed. She dragged a hand over her face. "I just . . . can't always do spontaneous. And if I say no, I need you to be okay with that."

"Okay," Mrs. Mason said softly.

"Okay." Ivy backed up a step. "I can go? I'll see you guys at the show?"

"Should I be going?" Mrs. Mason asked tentatively.

"Mom, yes," Ivy said. "Yes, I want you to come. If you want to come. No pressure."

Mrs. Mason smiled, and Mr. Mason nodded. "We'll be there," he said. "And we'll talk more later."

Ivy grabbed her coat, and we ran out the door. "That was an unexpected delay," she said. "I hope we still have enough time."

"We're going to have to run," I said, ducking down to tighten up my laces.

My partner laughed as she dragged me toward the garage. "You are forgetting something," she said. "We have access to some super speedy wheels, remember?"

Tank stood proudly in the corner, metal gleaming, ready and raring to be called up for duty. "As much faith as I have in Tank's super speediness, Ivy," I said. "I left Blue at home for stealth purposes so we're still down a ride."

"I don't know what you'd do without me and my amazing problem-solving skills, Howard," Ivy said. "Don't worry. Tank's got us covered."

A minute later, I found myself careening down Ivy's driveway, perched on Tank's handlebars. "We can't solve the case if we don't make it to the school, Ivy," I yelled over my shoulder.

"It'll be fine," Ivy said. "I've gotten much better at steering." We wobbled dangerously close to the edge of the sidewalk. "Just have to account for the extra weight."

I tightened my grip, keeping the edges of my coat tucked tight between my legs. She patted me on the head, knocking at the borrowed helmet and laughed. "Watch out for your sash!"

The belt of my coat whipped dangerously in the wind, veering closer to Tank's spokes. I risked my hold on my perch to grab the loose end and stuff it into my pocket. We crested the hill on Maple Street, and Ivy whooped while we picked up speed. As a steep decline unfolded before me, I began to wonder if planning to arrive in one piece had been optimistic.

I hummed under my breath, trying to distract myself from imminent death.

"Howard," Ivy called out. "Are you singing the new sneak theme?"

My jaw clamped shut as I realized that was exactly what I was doing. Her cackles rounded out the soundtrack for the rest of the ride.

Chapter Twenty-Four

I vy and I pulled up to the school. I spilled out onto the ground, nearly kissing it in relief as Ivy locked up Tank. "People aren't meant to travel at that speed, Ivy," I said.

My partner shrugged. "I see a hill, I'm going to take advantage of it." She waved at our crew as they walked up. "Besides, we're totally on time so go team!"

I ignored the smirks as I stood up and straightened my coat. Arriving intact was the first step. Time to get down to business. Ivy and I filled everyone in on the events of the day including the revelation of Leyla's double-agent status.

The uproar was instantaneous.

"She turned on us?" Miles shook his head. "To help *Parker?*"

Ellis opened her mouth and closed it again, shock robbing her of any words.

"Did she help him hurt Audrey II?" Scotty asked. His voice was tight with outrage.

Carl shot him a pointed look before turning to us. "What about Bradley? Did she help him with that too?"

Ivy and I exchanged a glance. "We're not sure how involved she's been," Ivy said. "There's still a lot we don't know."

"Why are we waiting here then?" Ashi darted toward the school, and I grabbed her sleeve to reel her back in. Wouldn't do to run headfirst into this mess.

"We need some answers," Ellis finally said. "How could she do this?" Everyone else nodded as Ellis's words set off a fresh wave of outcries.

I held up my hands, trying to quiet the crew's chatter. "Let's not waste time cursing Leyla for her sudden and debatably inevitable betrayal."

"Sorry," Miles snarked. "Some of us haven't had as long to wrap our head around this since we're just being told about it now."

"We only found out about it ourselves a couple of hours ago," I said.

"Well," Ashi held up a finger, "technically you knew about it yesterday."

"No, we knew there was a mole yesterday, but we didn't know it was Leyla until today," I said. "Are we going to argue about details, or are we going to figure out what to do next?"

Carl snorted from where he stood on the other side of the circle. I shot a look at him as he raised his eyebrows at me. "Now you want our input?"

"Yeah," Miles said, getting steamed up all over again. "Let's talk about that. You didn't even bother telling us about the fact that there was a possible leak? What happened to working together as a team?"

Ivy hummed and looked away, leaving me to take a crack at that one. "Listen," I said. "We couldn't be sure who it was. I had to make the right call for the agency and the case."

"You didn't trust us to tell you the truth," Scotty said quietly, shoulders hunched as he stuffed his hands in his pockets.

"It's not like you haven't lied to me before." We didn't have the time for me to be delicate about this. If they wanted to talk it out, we'd talk it out, but it was gonna be quick. Who knew what Parker was up to right now. "Asking you straight out would have ended up with everyone swearing they weren't the mole and the actual mole getting tipped off that we knew. The element of surprise was the only edge we had. We couldn't afford to lose it."

"You don't know that," Miles said, shaking his head. "That's what you think would've happened, but you don't *know*, and that's the worst part. Maybe if you'd trusted us, even if it tipped Leyla off, we could have worked together to figure this out."

"Miles is right," Carl said before I could jump in with a retort. "But it's more than today. If you'd let us help before, things wouldn't have gotten this bad. If you'd let even one of us come with you for backup on Monday, we'd have caught Parker in the act."

"And stopped Bradley from getting hurt." Ellis crossed her arms, giving me a hard stare.

"I'm more than aware of the mistakes I've made in this case," I said. "I didn't think we were keeping track."

"Let's all take a breath," Ivy said before Miles cut in.

"If the mistakes we made in the past are keeping you from trusting us," he said, "Why should we trust you? How do we know you'll work with the team and not run off when you think you have a better plan? Why is your decision the final one?"

"I don't—I wouldn't—" I couldn't find the words to make this right.

"Do you even want to work with us?" Scotty asked, unable to meet my eyes.

"Yes." The answer burst out, and the truth of it hit me in the chest. "Yes, I want to work with you guys."

Carl nodded slowly. "Will you *let* us work with you?"

I thought back to my talk with Eileen. It wasn't just about giving everyone a job. It was trusting them to do it. And it had to go both ways. "Yes," I said. "If you still want to."

Carl and Miles exchanged glances with the rest of the group as I waited out their verdict.

"Yeah," Carl said as the rest of them nodded.

"Okay," Ivy said, clapping her hands together. "Glad we got that sorted out. Question is—what do we do now? I vote in favor of saving the play, obviously."

Ellis pointed at Ivy, stabbing at the air vigorously. "Yes. And stopping Parker."

"Yeah," Ashi said, leaping up center of the circle. "And making him pay for everything he's done by grinding him into the dirt and kicking his butt."

She lowered her fists as we stared at her. "Or let teachers

deal with him. That also works. We can work on that part of the plan."

"Ideas on how we go about this?" I threw it out there, letting the crew take the lead.

"We go in teams," Carl said. "Split up and look for Parker."

"But keep in touch," Ivy said, waving her phone. "No one should be confronting him without backup. Especially you, Ellis."

"Me?" Ellis looked up, startled at being singled out.

"We think you're his most likely target," I said, explaining what we'd overheard from Leyla's phone call. "Based on what I saw from yesterday's rehearsal, he doesn't appreciate sharing the spotlight. It's all or nothing for him at this point."

Ivy pulled a crumpled piece of paper out of her pocket and checked over our sketch of the school. "Carl and Miles, why don't you take the back entrance? Ellis can go with Scotty and Ashi in the front by the office. Howard and I are going in the other side by the gym."

"Now spread out," Ashi said, flashing her hands through the air. She beamed. "I've always wanted to be the one to say that."

Assignments dealt with, we headed into the school. Ivy and I were tackling the stage area for our search zone. I wasn't keen on returning to the scene of my downfall, but it was the most likely area for Parker to show up, and I wanted us as the first line of defense. If any of us were going to get caught, odds were good on Parker blowing the whistle. Better it be me than anyone else on the team. In for a penny, in for an extended suspension.

We slid in the side door and tiptoed down the hall. I snuck a look around the corner, holding Ivy back with one arm.

"What is it?" She whispered, chin hooked over my shoulder.

"Problem," I said.

She craned her neck around to see Mrs. Pamuk and Mrs. Rodriguez talking in the hallway. "Wait them out?"

"Not much choice." It wasn't like I could lift up my collar and sneak by. The hallway didn't provide much in the way of cover, and I couldn't risk getting spotted by either of them. They'd yank me into the office, calling my folks on speed dial. Case closed indefinitely.

The door to the gym opened, and Ivy and I pressed close to the wall, eyes sharp as we watched from our corner.

"Howard, look," Ivy gasped quietly.

Parker stepped out into the hall and joined Mrs. Pamuk in her chat with Mrs. Rodriguez. I strained forward, unable to make out any words. Great. If Parker was sticking to their sides, we had no shot at him.

I debated storming over there and telling them everything we had on Parker. Could be worth whatever punishment I'd get for being on school property. But all we had was circumstantial evidence and our own hunches. Not enough to guarantee he'd go down. And no way to tell if he'd already set a trap for Ellis. If we took him in now and he refused to crack, we could be leaving her open for anything to happen.

No. We'd come up with a plan, and it was a good one. I couldn't let the crew down by changing it now. The only choice was to sit this out and wait for Parker to make a move.

If he'd ever stop talking.

After ten minutes, Mrs. Rodriguez finally departed for the office leaving Parker and Mrs. Pamuk alone in the hall. Parker murmured something to Mrs. Pamuk before darting back into the gym. And Mrs. Pamuk—

"Oh, crud," Ivy said, pulling me back from the wall.

Mrs. Pamuk was headed our way. We dashed down the hallway, looking for an open door. Ivy pushed open the closest one, hauling me in behind her. I held my breath, one hand pressed against the door, listening to her footsteps coming closer. They stopped outside the door.

"Leyla." Mrs. Pamuk's voice drifted through the vent at the bottom of the door. "I wanted to talk to you about the setup for the box office tonight."

"Sure thing, Mrs. P," Leyla answered. I stiffened at the sound of her voice, inching closer to listen. Ivy pawed at my back, and I waved her off.

Leyla—out there talking business as usual while Parker was running amok. Casually chatting away with Mrs. Pamuk while we were trapped and powerless to help our crew until the coast was clear.

The crew.

We had to let them know we were stuck. I turned to my partner. "Ivy—"

"Ivy?"

Her face was turning a disturbing purple color, one hand pinching her nose.

"What's wrong? What's going on?" I whispered.

She flailed a hand around the room, and I took in our surroundings. The boys' bathroom. "*Oh*," I said, finally getting a good whiff of the unique bouquet of aromas. "Welcome to the reason we don't normally meet in here."

"This is disgusting," she hissed, pulling the collar of her shirt up over her nose. "We have to get out of here."

"And walk right into Leyla and Mrs. Pamuk?" I jerked my head at the blocked exit behind us. "We're not going anywhere. We have to let the others know."

Ivy groaned and whipped out her phone. "And Parker's already in the gym. If they can get there, they might still be able to catch him." Her fingers flew as she tapped out a message.

A part of me wanted to stop her—tell her to wait until we were clear to move too. I wanted the chance to face off with Parker and prove I could take him down myself. A few days of solitude had left me with a nicely rounded out grudge. But an overzealous ego was what got us in this situation in the first place, and revenge wasn't in the cards tonight—not with everything we had laying on the line. I'd made a promise, and we couldn't afford to fail. That meant using every inch of brains and brawn we had at our disposal.

"Miles and Carl have a clear route to the gym," Ivy whispered, peering at her screen. "Ellis, Scotty, and Ashi aren't far behind."

Taking down Parker was the goal, and whoever got the opportunity had to take it.

"Tell them to be careful," I said. "We have no idea what he's setting up. I don't want anyone else getting hurt." I strained to listen in on the conversation continuing on the other side of the door. "Hopefully we'll be there soon."

Ivy and I stood behind the door, stock–still, as we waited for Mrs. Pamuk and Leyla to finish up their conversation. Short bursts of air hit my ear as Ivy tried to take shallow breaths through her mouth.

"Nope," she muttered. "Not any better."

I held up a finger to my lips, shushing her as I tried to hear what was happening in the hallway.

"I can taste it now," she whispered. "It's coating my tongue."

After one final agonizing minute, the voices stopped and the click of Mrs. Pamuk's heels faded as she walked away. I cracked open the door to see if the coast was clear. No one in sight except for a flash of blue hair disappearing around the corner. I signaled to give Ivy the go ahead, and she shoved me back toward the door, fumbling to fling it open herself when I took too long. She stumbled out into the hall, gasping for air. "I will never be the same," she said. "My DNA has been fundamentally corrupted by that stench."

"Come on," I said, pulling her upright. "There's still time. We gotta move."

Ivy and I raced around the corner in time to see Leyla

slide though the backstage door. Now was our chance. I loped down the hallway, Ivy hot on my heels, and grabbed the door before it could click shut.

Leyla whirled around as we slipped in behind her.

"Howard," she said. "Couldn't stay away? This is a bold move, even for you."

"My bag's full of tricks, Leyla," I said. "Gonna use the next one on Parker, and you're going to help me."

"And why would I do that?" she scoffed. But even through the dim light of the stairwell, I saw her hand tremble as she pushed her hair back. The slight twitch in her jaw. Heard the slight crack in her words.

"Because you're in too deep," I said. "Whatever scheme you agreed to, that's not what Parker's up to, is it?"

"I don't—" Leyla's voice caught. "I have no idea what he's up to." She sighed. "But I know it can't be good."

"Can't be any worse than what I just experienced." Ivy pushed forward and started up the stairs. "Get on board or get out of the way, Leyla," she said. "We're ending this before that curtain comes up."

Leyla squared her shoulders as my partner breezed past. "I want the exclusive," she said.

She got points for nerve but lost them on timing. "Think

we can haggle about official quotes after we take down Parker?" I prodded her toward the stage, ignoring her huffs.

I crept along the floorboards, willing the ancient wood not to creak. Best not to alert anyone to our presence in case the team hadn't caught Parker yet. I squinted through the dim light. Aside from Ivy shuffling up ahead and Leyla to my right, the stage was empty and the gym was still.

The silence sent an uneasy chill up my spine. Had Parker given our crew the slip? Hard feat when it's five against one. No. He was a slippery snake, but he wouldn't duck out without taking his shot. Parker was here somewhere. Biding his time. Waiting to get the drop on us.

A crash rang out from the far side of the stage.

"Prop room," Ivy whispered.

We tensed up, racing forward when the shouts began. I couldn't hold back a grin as I recognized the voices.

Fool me once, shame on you.

Fool me twice, face the wrath of an entire detective agency.

Chapter Twenty-Five

I hung onto the doorway of the props room, panting after my sprint across the stage. Ivy and Leyla slammed into my back, and we all gaped at the scene unfolding before us.

A red-faced Ellis was sitting on top of Parker, ranting, as Miles and Scotty attempted to keep her from pummeling him. Carl ducked Ellis's flailing hands while he tried to pull Parker out from under her. Ashi stood to the side, well out of the way of the danger zone. Her eyes lit up when she spotted us.

"Hey, guys," she said, picking her way through the props strewn across the floor. "Look who we found."

Leyla shoved me aside and stalked into the room. "What's going on?"

"What's going on?" Ellis looked up at her, snarling. "What's going on is that Parker tried to *kill* me."

The three of us turned to look at Parker in shock. He used the momentary distraction to scramble out of Ellis and Carl's grasp. "Leyla," Parker gasped for air as he stumbled to his feet, "you're my witness. They attacked me." He lurched forward and grabbed her arm. "Go get Mrs. Pamuk. Right now."

Ivy and I stood in the doorway, tensed and ready. I wasn't sure which side Leyla was going to fall on in this fight. If Parker still held some sway with her, things were going to get messy quick. No one was leaving here until we got the truth.

"Is this what you agreed to, Leyla?" I said softly.

She stared down at the fingers gripping her arm before meeting Parker's eyes. "What do you mean he tried to kill you?" Leyla asked Ellis as she yanked herself out of Parker's clutches.

"Show them." Ellis jerked her chin at Carl, and he pulled a small glass vial out of his pocket.

"We walked in on him putting a few drops of this in Ellis's water bottle," Carl said as he tossed it over to me. I caught the vial and held it up to inspect with Ivy. Inside was a light brown liquid that swirled around sluggishly. Some sort of oil maybe. I unscrewed the lid and took a sniff. Took another for good measure. "Smells like . . . *cinnamon*. Is this cinnamon extract?" The implications of that hit me as I looked back at Ellis. She stood there, grim-faced and nodding.

"A few drops would have been more than enough to trigger a reaction," Ellis said.

"What the heck, Parker?" Leyla stomped up to him, poking at his chest. "This is serious. What's wrong with you?"

"Oh, please." Parker rolled his eyes. "You told me it was a mild allergy. It was just to take her out of the show. Sore throat. A few hives. Not a big deal."

"Very big deal," Carl said, glaring at Parker and Leyla darkly. "You don't mess around with stuff like that."

I turned to Leyla. "Why were you telling Parker about Ellis's cinnamon allergy? You said he was up to something," I said. "Did you know about this?"

Leyla shook her head furiously. "No. *No*," she said. "It was ages ago. He kept asking about everyone early on, likes and dislikes sort of thing. I figured he was fishing, but I never—" She waved a hand through the air. "Never dreamed he'd do something like this." Leyla grabbed the vial and shook it in Parker's face. "This would have sent her to the hospital, you moron. What were you thinking?"

"That I would do whatever it takes," Parker said, snapping out the words. "When did you lose your nerve? I thought we were a team. Or are you picking and choosing your dirty work now?"

"Why, Leyla?" The fight was draining out of Ellis as she looked at her friend. "Howard said you've been working with Parker? Is that true?"

Leyla took a deep breath, staring down at the vial in her hand, fingers clenching reflexively around it. "It started with the costumes," she said in a rush. "My mom was late picking me up after rehearsal, and I saw Parker leave the school. He was carrying garbage bags that were jam-packed."

"He threw them out?" Ashi gasped.

"No one can prove what was in those bags," Parker said, inching toward the door. Carl grabbed him by the collar and hauled him back.

"I have pictures of him doing it," Leyla confirmed.

"You didn't *stop* him?" The note of betrayal in Ashi's voice was gut piercing.

"I wasn't 100 percent sure what had been in the bags until word got out about the costumes the next morning," Leyla said. "I confronted him about it and used the pictures to get him to let me in on his plan."

Parker jerked in Carl's hold. "This is ridiculous," he said. "Hearsay. Gossipmongering for a cut-rate middle school blog."

Carl placed a hand over Parker's mouth.

"And then you didn't go to a teacher because . . ." I prompted Leyla.

She looked at me like I'd asked her in French. "The story."

"*Leyla,*" Ivy said. "Are you kidding me right now?"

"What? Listen," Leyla paced the width of the tiny room. "You all know that nothing happens in this town—or it didn't until Howard started taking cases."

I took a step back. "Don't pin this on me."

"Your work is newsworthy." Leyla said it like it was a precious thing. "But people eat it up when things go wrong. A fluff piece never gets as many hits as a total catastrophe. And let's face it, with you, things usually go at least a little bit off the rails."

I glared at Miles when he began to nod.

"I thought it would work out in the end," Leyla said. "It usually does. Like the dognapping case with Spartacus. I figured I was helping to keep things interesting."

"Thanks for that," I said. "Didn't hurt that you could record it all for your blog."

"That was exactly the point," Leyla scoffed. "Have you seen my numbers lately?"

"I can't believe this," Miles said. "You've been helping him behind our backs for *ratings*?" He leaned back against the shelves, eyes wide in disbelief. "And you never once thought 'Hey, maybe this isn't a good idea'? You were fine with Howard getting suspended? With Bradley getting hurt?"

"No." Leyla pointed a shaking finger at Miles before turning to Parker. "Bradley was never supposed to be hurt," she said flatly as Parker glared at her, mumbled words muffled by Carl's hand. "Parker told me he was only going to frame Howard for damaging the set. Not push it over on you guys."

I looked over at my partner in disbelief. "This story keeps getting better."

"Be honest," Leyla snapped. "You always manage to get in trouble, but you never let it stick. I thought you could wiggle your way out of a little frame job."

"I'm honored by your faith in me," I said. "But it's misplaced. I couldn't have made it through this one without the crew. And we're not done yet so you've got to decide, and you better make it quick. Are you going to help us finish this job? We could use the backup."

"Oh, that's so touching," Parker sneered, wrestling out

of Carl's hold. "It's still my word against yours. You have no proof." He kept a wary eye on the rest of us as he held up a hand to stave off any further attack. "You're not even supposed to be here. In fact, you're the one who's suspended for tampering with the play. I haven't done anything wrong. Imagine my shock when I came in here and found you tampering with Ellis's water bottle. I tried to stop you, but of course your little friends stuck up for you. Who do you think they're going to believe? You have nothing, Howard."

I didn't bother stopping the smirk tugging at my lips. "I think they're going to believe Ivy's video." My partner moved in closer, holding up her phone to capture every bit of the exchange.

Parker craned his neck to look around Leyla. "You're filming this?" He yanked his arms out of Carl's hold, lunging toward Ivy. She leapt back, keeping her phone in hand, and kicked out with one leg. Parker went down as she cracked a solid one on his right knee. Scotty and Ashi were on him in an instant, sitting on his chest while pinning his arms and legs. "Get off of me," he screamed, thrashing uselessly on the floor. "No! This show wouldn't exist if it wasn't for me. It's been carried by one person. One star," he said. "Mrs. P has to know how much *I've* been doing. All she can talk about is

Ellis. I'm the best actor this school has ever seen, and that's never going to change."

"Pretty sure that's changing today," I said.

"You guys good?" Ashi and Scotty nodded as they kept their focus on our captive.

"Yup." Ivy turned off her video and popped her phone in her pocket. "I taught them that move," she said, pointing at Ashi and Scotty with a smile.

"And I'm sure Parker's happy you did," I said. "How are we doing for time? We need to get this mess cleaned up."

Miles let out a low whistle as he checked. "Not good. Mrs. Pamuk is going to be here any second. We need to get you out of sight if we're going to keep you out of trouble."

"I'm going to press charges," Parker said, panting as he struggled. "You are all going to be arrested and barred from this stage. For life."

"Okay, Carl, bag up the evidence." I tossed him the vial of oil, and Leyla handed him the water bottle. "We need to immobilize Parker."

"Like tie him up?" Ivy's eyes gleamed with a mischievous light. "I can do that," she said. "I know where the good duct tape is." She ran out of the room with a shouted promise to return.

Leyla bent down and started rummaging through Parker's pockets. "Aha." She straightened up and waved around her prize with a flourish. "Found his phone. We can look for more evidence."

"I better grab that," Carl said, taking it gently out of her grasp. Leyla started to argue, and I held up a hand.

"You're not exactly a neutral party at this point, Leyla. We don't know what he has on there and leaving it in your care isn't the best bet. Be peeved if you want, but maybe think about who you join up with next time."

Ivy ran back in the room with her roll of tape and some rope. "Got it," she said. "Hold him steady, kids, I'm going in."

"No, no, no." Parker wiggled furiously. "Listen. Listen," he said. "No one has to know any of this happened. We can work out a story. Howard, I'll make sure you get cleared for the stage thing. Just give me tonight. Please."

"Sorry, Parker," I said, ripping off a strip of tape. "Looks like you already took your final bow."

Ivy groaned as she grabbed Parker's kicking legs. "Howard. Really?"

"No? No good? How about 'it's curtains for you, pal'?" I grinned at my partner.

Ashi let out a little shriek as Parker tried to fling her off. "Less joking, more taping!"

Between Ivy, Miles, Carl, Scotty, Ashi, and me, we managed to get Parker's feet and wrists bound tight and enough tape on his mouth to intercept any further protests.

"Leyla," Ivy said. "You should grab Mrs. Pamuk before she gets here and keep her distracted as long as you can. Tell her you need help with tickets or something."

Spinning on her heel, Leyla left with a stiff nod. At least she was willing to work on gaining back some reliability points. The rest of us were left in the tiny room with Parker and his muffled shouts.

Scotty shifted on his rocky seat of Parker's kicking legs. "Now what?"

Chapter Twenty-Six

I vy sprang into action. "Okay," she said. "We're down a Seymour, we need a Seymour. Ellis, you know the part, right?"

"I know all the parts," Ellis said. "But I can't be Audrey *and* Seymour."

"Ivy, you know the Audrey part," Ashi piped up. "You've basically been Ellis's understudy. You could totally do it!"

My partner mulled that over, staring seriously down at her shoes. "Yeah, I could," she said. "I can do that. But what about my part? We need someone who knows the choreography."

Ashi grinned, pressing her glasses up the bridge of her nose. "Someone who knows the choreography? Someone who's been helping me run through the steps for weeks and probably knows them better than I do? Someone who knows all the words to all the songs?"

"Yes, Ashi," Ivy said. "Someone like that would be ideal."

"Oh, hey, Scotty," Ashi said, hopping over to the stricken-looking blond. "Remember that time when you helped me learn everything and I said you would rock being in this play?"

"Ashi, nooooo," Scotty whispered.

"Ashi, yes! *Scotty*, yes!" she said. "We're going to knock their socks off. I already know the perfect costume for you." Ashi hauled Scotty off to the storage room the costumes had been stowed away in.

"That covers the roles," Ivy said. "But we still need to stash Parker somewhere."

Parker grunted his objections to this part of the plan as Miles and Carl held him still between them.

"We need to put him somewhere no teachers are going to come across him," I said. "Can't risk anyone finding him backstage. The bathrooms are out. If I'd known we were going to have to stash a body, I'd have asked Pete to unlock the closet."

"We wouldn't have been able to carry him through the halls anyway," Ivy said. "Someone might see, and we can't risk you being seen either."

"Audrey II," Ellis shouted suddenly.

We paused our brainstorming session to give her room to elaborate.

"Someone needs to operate Audrey II during the play," she said. "That's supposed to be Scotty's job, but if we're putting him on stage—"

I shook my head. "Ellis, focus," I said. "We need to figure out this problem first, not who's going to be hanging out in the giant plant—oh."

"And he gets it," Ellis cheered.

She walked Ivy and me over to the papier-mâché monstrosity sitting in the far corner of the stage. Leafy vines draped over the top and trailed down the sides. The wide mouth hung open at a crooked angle. It looked big enough for two, but it was going to be close quarters.

"What about when the plant eats people," Ivy said. "How are they going to fit in with the two of them already in there?"

I stopped my examination of the slightly lopsided prop to stare at my partner. "The plant eats people?"

"Did you pay any attention during rehearsals?" Ivy snorted.

"I paid plenty of attention to the case I was trying to solve," I said. "The rest was just soundtrack. Back to the problem at hand, does this plant have an extension or are we officially out of plans?"

"I'm running the lights," Carl said. "I could turn them down so that whoever's getting eaten can poke their head in the plant and then duck offstage while it's dark."

"That'll work," Scotty said, struggling his way into a sequined shirt as he returned to the group. "Miles is doing all of Audrey II's lines from the sound booth, but Howard, you're going to have to operate the plant."

"Howard has to what?"

Ivy patted me on the shoulder with a grin. "Just move the mouth up and down when you hear Miles's voice, and you'll be fine."

"There's got to be another way," I said, racking my brain.

"We have to get moving," Ellis said, looking at her watch. "Leyla's not going to be able to stall Mrs. Pamuk much longer. We're running out of time."

Carl and Miles manhandled Parker over to Audrey II. He fought against them every step of the way. As they tried to duck his head into the plant, we heard a scrape and a gasp from the other side of the stage.

Everyone turned to see Nina, the stage manager, standing by the curtains, staring at our predicament. Parker growled at her through his gag, renewing his attempts to break free. Nina took a step forward and then hesitated.

She shot a look over at Ellis. "There's a good reason?"

"It's Parker," Ellis snapped. "There's a million good reasons. Take your pick."

Nina pursed her lips, tapping her fingers along her clipboard. "Got his role covered?"

"Plans have been made," Ivy said.

"Then that's all I need to know," Nina said, backing away. "Mrs. Pamuk'll be here in five. Get sorted before then. And *don't* screw up your cues."

She hustled offstage while Carl and Miles returned to stuffing Parker inside the plant. After a brief struggle that left no one's dignity intact, they managed to fit him in without bloodshed.

Leyla rushed in, darting through the closed curtains. "Howard, your parents," she hissed. "They're here. They're looking for you."

Right. I was supposed to check in about twenty minutes ago. "Did you talk to them?"

"They asked me where you were," she said. "I told them I hadn't seen you, and then I lost track of them. I was too busy trying to keep Mrs. Pamuk distracted. You should get out of here."

I definitely needed to get out of sight, but I wasn't

abandoning this case. Squaring my shoulders, I resigned myself to my fate. "Guess I'm getting in the plant."

"Your Broadway debut." Ivy began to giggle. "I can't believe we're doing this." A hysterical note danced around the edges of her laugh.

"Believe it," I said. "Because you guys have gotta sell it. We can't have Mrs. Pamuk poking around once she gets here."

Ivy closed her eyes and shook out her hands. "Okay," she said, looking back at me. "We can do this."

I poked at her shoulder. "Knock 'em dead, partner."

"Break a leg," Miles called out.

"Still too soon." I ducked my head to climb in after Parker. Scotty rearranged the fabric over the opening to hide us from view. Enough light filtered in from the stage that I could see Parker sitting beside me, squirming against his ties.

"You and I need to talk," I said.

He scoffed and focused on his task at hand.

"The play is starting any minute," I whispered to Parker as he glared at me through the dim light filtering through the fabric covering Audrey II's mouth. The chaotic sounds of backstage were clear as Mrs. Pamuk discovered the absence of one of her leads.

"Where is Parker?" she whisper-yelled. "*Where. Is. Parker?*"

"About that," Ivy said, working fast to smooth things over.

Parker scowled as my partner talked, and I held his bound wrists tight in case he was thinking of making a break for it. "You can bust out of here," I said, reading the intent clear in his eyes. "But then everyone will know what you've been up to."

He rolled his eyes, the huff coming through loud and clear behind the tape covering his mouth.

"Yes, people are going to find out anyway," I agreed. "But there's a difference between us telling Mrs. Pamuk and Mrs. Rodriguez about this and telling the whole town. There's still a chance here for you to save face."

Parker stilled, abandoning his search for an escape to listen to my pitch.

"You leave now and we'll plaster the story everywhere. You think you had a hard time getting a role at your school this year?" His eyes widened at that. "Oh, yeah, I know all about your chorus-fueled hissy fit. I have spies everywhere, Parker."

Things on the stage had quieted down. Ivy and Ellis must have convinced Mrs. Pamuk to go with their plan. Not that she had any other options. We only had a few minutes before showtime.

"Nobody's gonna want a saboteur in their company. You

want a chance at the spotlight again, I'm going to need you to play ball. Keep quiet and help me with the cues. Deal?"

The rage burning in Parker's eyes sputtered out and he nodded stiffly. We shook hands as best we could with his tied together. Everything went dark as the lights came down. It was happening. We were surrounded by shuffling noises as everyone came out on stage and found their spots. With a whoosh, the curtains were pulled back and the lights came back up.

Showtime.

I'd missed out on the full run-throughs due to my undeserved suspension. Despite the cramped quarters, I'd still landed one of the best seats in the house. Parker and I squished together to view the action through the gauzy material inside Audrey II's mouth. Musicals had never been my bag. Most likely because they were Eileen's jam of choice. But sitting there while my friends belted out their numbers, I found myself bopping along and enjoying the show. Scotty was doing a surprisingly good job holding up his end of the chorus alongside the ball of energy that was Ashi. Ellis was nailing her part. I ignored Parker's pouting when she belted out his solo.

And Ivy.

Ivy was amazing.

Not that I expected anything less. My partner dove into all of our jobs with intense enthusiasm and this was no different. She had the audience eating out of the palm of her hand.

Parker and I stumbled through our part. We were nearly stacked on top of one another inside of Audrey II, leaving precious little room to maneuver. Parker smacked me with his bound hands as every cue came up. Hopefully there was enough action onstage to distract from the fact that the botanical co-star was always half a beat behind.

During the bows, Parker turned to me and gestured to his mouth, muffled noises coming through the tape.

"You want me to take that off?"

He nodded eagerly as I sat back on my heels, considering. We weren't out of the woods yet, and losing one of our safety measures seemed an unwise turn to take.

Parker widened his eyes, silent pleas coming through loud and clear. I shook my head. I'd seen this movie before. Taking off the gag was the first step in prisoner escape 101. "No dice, Parker," I said. "We're sitting tight until that curtain closes."

My captive leaned in close. The saddest-sounding whine I'd ever heard escaped from behind his gag. I took a quick peek outside. How many more bows could they possibly take?

Pathetic noises were still coming from my left, filling our cramped quarters with its own soundtrack of sorrow. "Can it," I said. "You're not tied up because you're the good guy here. You brought this situation on yourself."

"Mmmph pfrum mhhhm pfhum," Parker said.

"I could lie and say I respect your point of view, but the answer's still no." I tightened up his wrist ties just in case.

"MMMPH PFRUM."

Growling, I ripped the tape off of Parker's mouth, slapping a hand over it instead. "When I remove this hand," I said. "Whatever you so desperately have to say better be real interesting."

"I'm sorry," Parker whispered as soon as his lips were freed. "I was so angry and . . . and disappointed. I let everything get out of hand. We never had anything like this when I was here. When I didn't get cast at my school and I found out about the production here, I was so mad. I kept missing my chances. All I could think about was being on stage again." He nodded out toward the lights in front of us. "Hearing that. Just for me."

"That's—"

"I know, it's no excuse," Parker said "What I did was terrible. There's no way to justify my behavior. I should be thanking you and your friends for stopping me when you did."

I sat back on my heels, caught off guard by Parker's confession. "Really?"

"No, you idiot." He smirked. "It's called acting." He swung his arms up and caught me across the temple. Bright spots clouded my vision as my ears rang from the blow. Parker shoved me back with his elbow then leveraged himself up to a crouch. Before I could grab him, he propelled himself out through the mouth of Audrey II and onto the stage.

A lurching wave of gasps came from the audience as people noticed his sudden arrival. This had turned sideways quick. That tricky miscreant had been untying his shoes during his little confession, and I hadn't noticed a thing. I didn't know who was the bigger idiot. The uproar from outside increased as Parker began ranting from the stage.

Parker.

Parker was the bigger idiot.

Resting my head in my hands, I sighed. A public venue. Multiple witnesses. Probable future accusations of kidnapping. The odds of this situation turning in my favor were dropping and picking up speed. But that was my crew out there, and I wasn't about to let them face the music alone. However off-key things may be.

Taking a deep breath, I dove out onto the stage.

Chapter Twenty-Seven

"**T**his isn't an encore," Parker screamed. "This is a conspiracy!"

Our delinquent star rampaged across the stage as I struggled to worm my way out of our hideaway. Parker had managed to make his escape look sleek and effortless.

I did not. Dark, cramped, and under pressure were not ideal operating conditions. My roll dive came undone as I tangled in the foliage protruding from the giant plant. With a thump, I landed on the stage in an inelegant sprawl, narrowly missing taking out the three shocked chorus members standing beside Audrey II.

Another gasp spread through the audience. "And there's the ringleader." Parker's voice rang out from the speakers.

He was standing center stage, microphone clutched in his still bound hands. I peered through the bright spotlight, attempting to assess the situation. Ivy, Ellis, and the rest of the cast stood frozen while Mrs. Pamuk looked on in horror from behind the curtain. Parker stalked the front of the stage, the audience held in the grip of his rant.

"Howard Wallace and his friends attacked me and tied me up to stop my performance in this play tonight." He took a deep breath before bowing his head slightly to release it on a shaky sigh. "They have been sabotaging this play since day one." Parker let his voice crack a bit on that last line. The front row leaned forward in their seats.

Enough of this. I couldn't let Parker and his hack-job performance get the upper hand. Hands gripped under my arms as I struggled to right myself, helping to pull me to my feet. I looked over my shoulder to give Scotty and Ashi an appreciative nod.

Making my way to the front of the stage, I got a glimpse of my parents and Eileen sitting beside Ivy's family. My folks were watching me with a mixture of confusion and resignation. Eileen stared, eyes wide. *What are you doing*, she mouthed at me. Excellent question. Lillian waved from her seat beside a grinning Marvin while the rest of the audience blurred together in a sea of shocked faces and camera flashes.

"Here he comes," Parker said, the taunt twisting his lips. "Ready to tell more lies."

Mrs. Rodriguez was inching down the far side of the gym, creeping closer to the stage. If I was going to get a word in, now was the time. I grabbed the second microphone from the stand and glanced back at my partner. She shrugged. I nodded.

We were officially at the 'bluffing our way out of this' part of the plan.

"Good evening, everyone. My name is Howard, and I'm playing the role of Kidnapper Number One tonight." A small titter went through the front row. So far, so good.

"Tell them what you did, Howard," Parker said with a snarl.

"Tell them what *you* did," Ellis said, busting through the group of actors on the stage. A murmur went up as she grabbed the microphone out of my hand. "You tried to poison me! You could have *killed* me!"

"Okay, obviously the stress of a lead role is getting to you." Parker turned to the audience. "Not everyone can handle the spotlight."

"You've been behind everything." Ellis strode up to Parker, rage fueling the tide of words. "You wrecked the set, destroyed the costumes, hurt Bradley—and for what? A role in a middle school play that you had to *steal?*"

"The role I *deserved*," Parker hissed.

Ellis narrowed her eyes as she leaned in. "Not. With pitch. Like that."

Parker reared back, and Lillian's voice floated over the shocked whispering of the crowd. "I don't remember the play ending this way."

Ivy leapt forward and grabbed the microphone out of Ellis's hand. "My goodness," she said. "Poison, kidnapping, sabotage? That's just a taste of the excitement we're cooking up for you. Yes, the GMS Drama Club is working on an original play for next year's show and that was a little preview! Let's give these guys a hand."

The smattering of applause was enough cover for Ivy to turn to Scotty. "Curtains. *Curtains!*" she hissed. He sprang into action, pulling on the cord to haul the heavy red cloth across the stage, cutting us off from prying eyes.

Everyone took a breath. Carl and Miles emerged from the sound booth and pushed in beside Ivy and Ashi. Before we could break the silence, Mrs. Pamuk stepped forward, and the curtains twisted around as Mrs. Rodriguez fought her way backstage. They shared a weighted look, and Mrs. Rodriguez turned to pin us with a glare.

"Explain," she said. "Now."

Parker and Ellis started yelling at once. I considered getting back into the plant.

"I want short, concise sentences," Mrs. Rodriguez said, pointing an imperious finger. "Starting with you."

"Me?" Ashi squeaked from the far side of the circle. "Okay, uh, Parker has been sabotaging the play. He threw out the costumes."

"And trashed the sets," said Miles.

"He's the one who's responsible for Bradley getting hurt," Ivy said. "And helped blame Howard for it."

"*And* destroyed Audrey II," Scotty added. "Multiple times."

"He tried to give me an allergic reaction," Ellis said. "We caught him in the act."

"Parker, is this true?" Mrs. Pamuk rounded on him, frown lines etched deep between her brows.

"Complete lies," Parker said. "I've done nothing but try to help. Where is their proof? Are you going to take their word against mine?"

"Proof, proof, proof," I said, searching my pockets. "Oh,

right." I snapped my fingers. "We have a witness in the form of one Leyla Bashir who was both a willing and unwilling accomplice to your many crimes. We also have video evidence of us catching you in the act of trying to poison Ellis."

Scotty waved his phone. "I took a panoramic shot of the crime scene as well."

"There you go," I said. "Both widescreen and regular proof."

"And we have Parker's phone," Carl said, stepping forward to hand over the device. "There are some text messages you should take a look at."

Mrs. Rodriguez pinched the bridge of her nose, taking a deep breath in and letting it out slowly. "Okay," she said. "Parker, come with me, please. It would appear we have quite a bit to discuss. I will be speaking with all of you, including Miss Bashir. Keep your phones handy, I want to see everything you've collected." With that, she ushered Parker backstage and out into the hall.

The rest of us were left staring at each other.

"Really, guys?" Mrs. Pamuk burst out. "Really? This is what's been going on? You know I'm the teacher advisor here, right? I'm the adult. You're supposed to come to me with stuff like this. It's literally in the job description."

"We're sorry, Mrs. Pamuk," Ivy said. "We didn't know for sure what was going on at first, and then we thought it would be better to have proof so you could actually do something."

"Things may have gotten a little out of hand," I said.

"Did you realize that after the attempted poisoning or the kidnapping?" Mrs. Pamuk threw her hands up as she sighed. "Putting him in the plant?"

"It seemed like a good idea at the time," Scotty mumbled.

"It was more of a heat of the moment decision," Miles said.

"Speaking of," Mrs. Pamuk whirled back to face Ivy, "an original play, Ivy? What?"

Ivy buried her face in her hands, groaning. "I know. I know! I was trying to cover and that's what came out. It was the first thing that popped into my head."

"Well, I hope you have more ideas because you guys are writing it," Mrs. Pamuk said. "I suggest you start now." She sighed. "Excellent opening night, by the way."

Everyone perked up, grins sneaking in. "Yeah?" Ellis asked.

"Definitely," Mrs. Pamuk said. "You guys were great up there. Fantastic job on the leads, Ellis and Ivy. Great moves, Ashi and Scotty, I knew you had it in you. Miles, Carl—

you guys had backstage working like a well-oiled machine. Howard, for a first-time plant wrangler, you did good work. Considering everything else that was going on, I'd call it a definite success."

"Thanks, Mrs. P," Ellis said with a smile.

Mrs. Pamuk clapped her hands together. "Now, I believe there are some parents waiting to both congratulate and question you. Good luck." She herded us off the stage, and we all filed out into the hall.

As predicted, our parents were clustered in the hall waiting for our arrival, their expressions ranging from concerned to confused. Lillian was at the end looking downright gleeful.

"*Great* show, kids," she said. "Incredible stuff."

"Thanks, Grandma—Mom?" Ivy craned her neck to see her mom at the back of the crowd. "You came?"

"I said I would." Ivy's mom stepped forward as Ivy raised a brow at her. "Trying to keep my promises. And I'm glad I did. That was intense. Do all of your cases end so . . . dramatically?"

I scratched at my ear when all eyes turned to me and shrugged. "One in ten, maybe? Feels like more sometimes."

"Well," Mrs. Mason said. "I thought you handled yourselves well."

"Howard and I have gotten used to dealing with unexpected situations," Ivy said.

Mrs. Mason smiled as Lillian let out a cackle. "I'd like to hear about that sometime."

Ivy studied her mom before glancing over at her dad. "I was promised ice cream after the show," she said. "Do you maybe want to come with us?"

"I would like that very much," Mrs. Mason said softly.

They headed out, and Ashi, Miles, and Scotty followed with their parents. Carl dragged Marvin out after them despite his protests of wanting to see what happens next. I was left standing there with Eileen and my folks. Time to face the music.

"So," Pops said. "Want to tell us how you ended up with the best seat in the house?"

Chapter Twenty-Eight

By Monday, everyone in town knew about Friday's unexpected encore. Ivy kept me up to date with the reports, the latest being that Leyla was booted from her role as editor of the GMS blog. Leyla took the news in stride. She'd launched her personal news blog a few hours later with the first post an in-depth exposé on her fall from grace. With a masterful spin on her side of the story, she detailed how the pressure to succeed at a young age lead to her bad choices. Naturally.

It was touching.

It went viral.

There was no doubt Leyla was going to come out of this just fine.

My fate, however, had yet to be determined. Mrs. Rodriguez, still busy putting out fires, pushed our meeting back to the end of the day. At 3 p.m. sharp, my parents and I walked through the front door of the school. Shoulders back, chin up, ready to accept the many punishments deemed to fit my many crimes.

Mrs. Rodriguez ushered us into her office and took her seat behind the desk. She sat back in her chair, staring at her steepled fingers, and sighed. Seconds ticked by on the clock overhead. Sharp little snaps fighting to be heard through the thick silence that filled the tiny room.

I opened my mouth to break the ice when a squeeze of my hand forced me to bite back the words. Ma shook her head slightly, keeping her gaze focused forward as a pulsing muscle in her jaw kept time with the clock. Apparently, we were here to play the long game.

"I bought a two-year calendar."

My folks and I startled at Mrs. Rodriguez's words. She was staring at the back wall, a dreamy look in her eye. The hand gripping mine kept me from blurting out the five perfectly serviceable answers that popped into my brain. Instead, I gave a short nod of respectful neutrality. Hopefully.

"I marked down the day you graduate," Mrs. Rodriguez

said, finally cutting a look in my direction. "I think I'll buy a cake."

"Thank you?" The hand grip of death did not appreciate that response.

"The cake will be for me, Howard." Mrs. Rodriguez stared at me as she pulled a sheaf of papers out of a drawer and slapped them down on her desk. "These were waiting for me when I arrived today." She drummed her fingers over the pile. "Detailed statements from numerous students recounting their involvement in this mess and defending your actions."

That caught my attention. I scooted forward to try and catch a glimpse of the pages. Ivy's loopy writing was visible on top and the next page looked like Miles' chicken scratch. "Ivy Mason, Miles Fletcher, Carl Dean," Mrs. Rodriguez read out as she flipped through them. "Scotty Harris, Ashi Jenkins, Ellis Garcia. Leyla Bashir was kind enough to forward her . . . blog post." She stared over the top of her glasses at me. "These are all of your accomplices, correct?"

Did it count as snitching if they'd already ratted themselves out? It was hard to take the fall when everyone else was falling all over each other to do it first.

Mrs. Rodriguez was already pulling out another pile of paper. Small, pink squares covered in tidy printing. "Phone messages," she said. "From local businesses pledging ad space for next year's show. Here's a quote from Mr. Marvin Parsons. I believe you know him." Another sharp look in my direction. "He says 'If next year's show is half as exciting, count me down for a full page.' The rest of the message is him haggling the cost."

Pops coughed, muffling what sounded suspiciously like a laugh. "And then," he said, rallying. "Where does all of this leave Howard?"

"Your week of suspension is done. Aside from your classmates, Mrs. Pamuk also spoke up in your favor," Mrs. Rodriguez said. "Despite the fact that you've been expressly forbidden from investigating on school grounds, I cannot deny that if you hadn't intervened, Miss Garcia would most likely have ended up in the hospital." She kept a steady eye on me, taking my measure through the force of her gaze. Fingers crossed I wasn't falling short.

"I'm in communication with Parker's principal, and we are working together on appropriate disciplinary action. All GMS students involved in this situation, Howard included, are to serve a two week in-school detention, starting today." Mrs. Rodriguez paused, leaning forward in her chair. "I realize that I cannot watch you every minute that you're in my school,

Howard. And I can recognize that you have done some good. However, if you had come to us sooner, there is always the chance that we could have avoided this whole situation. The ban on investigations stands, but I will say that if you hear of a situation that requires a helping hand, my door is always open, and I'm not opposed to a little negotiation. Within reason."

"Understood," I said, nodding solemnly.

"When a serious problem comes up, you will always come to an adult."

"Of course," I agreed. I knew a peace treaty when it was smacking me over the head.

"If you could make it until summer vacation without ending up back here, that would be nice," she sighed.

"I will do my best, ma'am."

My parents shook hands with Mrs. Rodriguez and thanked her for her time and leniency. They herded me back out into the hallway before I had a chance to shake on it with her, but a verbal agreement was fine with me.

"Letters from all your friends, hm?" Pops rocked back on his heels with a grin. "Not too shabby a gang you've got going on there, kid."

"It'd be nice if he could find a group that *wouldn't* dive head first into trouble with him," Ma said.

"At least this way, he has backup," Pop said with a shrug. "But your mom has a point, Howard. I'm glad you've fallen in with a loyal crowd. That's great. But maybe, just for a little while, you guys could try doing some regular kid business. Bike rides and video games and stuff. Things that don't involve detention."

That pile of papers had been a surprising sight. I never expected everyone to stick up for me like that. Wasn't sure our team effort would carry forward after the curtains closed. It was a nice surprise.

And I didn't know what to make of that.

I tried to imagine meeting up with the crew for non-case-related activities. Pictured hanging out instead of giving out assignments. Ivy and I did that, but slotting everyone else into the equation took more work. Tried to see myself shooting hoops with guys.

Scratch that. Imagined eating cookies with Ashi while everyone else shot hoops.

Thought about not being Wallace of Wallace and Mason Investigations.

Not being the boss or the leader.

Just being Howard.

Maybe Pops was right. It was time for a change.

Chapter Twenty-Nine

Two weeks later, punishments served and detentions concluded, we met up at our usual Friday table at Mrs. H's. Miles, Carl, Ashi, Scotty, and Ellis all crammed into the booth while Ivy and I pulled up chairs on the end. I let out a satisfied sighed as I sat down. Everyone back together, sitting uncomfortably close at our favorite watering hole. Nice to have things back to normal.

Mrs. H came over to take our flurry of orders, waving away our money as we began pulling out wallets. "Today, it's on the house," she said, patting Ivy on the shoulder. "We missed you kids around here. Glad you're back in action."

"Mural looks great, by the way," I called after her. Toby Turner did surprisingly good work. And according to

Marvin, his *manager*, he was a rising Grantleyville star with new murals commissioned through the summer. Apparently, the only difference between public nuisance and public art installation was a paycheck.

Our orders arrived, and after everything was parceled out, Miles raised his mug. "To freedom," he said.

"To freedom," we echoed as we clinked our cups.

"Until four-thirty," Scotty added on. "My mom's still pretty cheesed about everything. She said I better not be late."

"My grandma said I could stay until five if I brought home lemon squares." Ivy grinned.

"Uncle Marv wants me to help clean out the shop," Carl said. "So we should stay here as long as possible."

I smiled as I took a sip, taking in the view. This was good. Having people. Having friends. Pops could be right about it being enough.

A shadow fell over our table, and the chatter petered out. I looked over my shoulder to see Leyla shuffling her feet as she stared hard at the vinyl tablecloth. "Hey, guys," she said. "How's, uh, how's everything going?"

"No one's tried to backstab us in the last couple of weeks so pretty good, I'd say." I raised my eyebrows at her, and she sighed.

"Listen," she said. "I'm sorry for how things went down. I never meant for anyone to get hurt."

"You mentioned that," Ellis said flatly. "In your blog post."

"Journalism is in my blood." Leyla shrugged. "I can't apologize for that. But lesson learned. I need to pick better partners."

"And commit fewer crimes," Scotty said around a mouthful of brownie.

"I didn't actually commit—" She cut herself off when we all stared. "Nope, yeah, you're right. No more shady business. Just the facts."

We'd barely had a chance to talk things out backstage. Leyla had given us her side of the story and helped bring down Parker, but the scales still felt unbalanced. Despite the courage it must have taken for Leyla to come over and speak to us, I couldn't bring myself to welcome her back with open arms. Not with the bitter taste of betrayal still fresh in my mouth. I wasn't that big of a person.

And I wasn't the only one.

"You broke our trust, Leyla," Ellis said. "It's going to take a lot more than helping to clean up a mess you made and a mediocre apology to come back from that."

"Bradley got hurt," Scotty said. "Howard could've been hurt, too."

"You should have come to us," Ivy said. "Not tried to capitalize on Parker's crimes."

Leyla's shoulders hunched in as she took in every word, nodding along with each rejection. My partner looked over to me for the final judgment, but I shook my head. This wasn't something for me to make an executive decision on. We all had to weigh in.

"I think," Carl said, measuring out each word carefully. "We've all made some bad decisions at one time or another. Ones that affected other people."

Ashi nodded. "Ones that we were allowed to make up for."

"As long as you want to work on it," Miles said, with a small smile in my direction.

I couldn't argue with any of that. "Up to you where it all goes from here," I said to Leyla.

She took a deep breath and let it out slowly. "I really am sorry," she said. "I know you don't trust me anymore and you probably never want to work with me again, but I hope someday you will. I hope you'll let me try." She ducked her head down to cover a sniff. "Anyway. I'm sorry. That's what I came here to say."

The rest of the group nodded as I looked around the table, some more reluctantly than others. "Okay," I said. "Apology accepted."

"Good," Leyla said. "Thanks. I'll just, uh, I'll see you around then." She turned to leave while we had a silent, rapid-fire discussion of blinks and head tilts.

"Leyla," Ellis called after her. "Pull up a chair." Leyla whirled around and grabbed a seat, dragging it over to the table. She and Ellis bumped shoulders when she plopped down beside her.

I fought back a grin at the picture we made as everyone settled back down again. Nice having the whole gang back together. And a perfect time to dive into the big news of the day.

"I'm glad everyone could make it today since we have some important business to discuss," I said, waiting for quiet to fall over the table. "I've decided to shut down Wallace and Mason Investigations."

That bomb sent a shockwave through the whole table. Scotty and Ashi's mouths dropped open, scattering crumbs everywhere. Carl glowered at me loudly from the other side of the table. Miles launched into a counter-argument despite not knowing any of the reasons. Leyla began typing on her phone before Ellis quietly forced her hand back down.

Ivy turned to face me, eyes wide with disbelief.

"Howard," she said, hurt coloring her voice. "What? Why?

Were you not even going to talk to me about this? I thought we were partners. What about everyone else?"

"Exactly," I said. That was the heart of it. "There's everybody else now. We're in new territory. The agency served its purpose, but it's also outlived it. I've got to change with the times and make a fresh start." If anything, working this case had made it crystal clear. I'd looked at it from every angle over the last few weeks. This was the best choice.

"You can't just decide something like this," Ivy said. "We get a say too."

"What happened to working together?" Miles exploded. "We should vote on this."

"All the nays," Ashi said. "Mark us down as a big no."

"No voting," I said, waving down their protests. Last thing we needed was to be kicked out before everyone finished their snacks. It was for the best. They'd see that. "No need to discuss what's already done. Wallace and Mason Investigations is officially closed."

The table was silent as the group absorbed the news. Self-preservation kicked in as I could spot the mutiny looming clear on the horizon. Time to move on. Quickly.

"That concludes the old business," I said, clapping my hands together. "I would like to formally call to order a new meeting for new business." I pulled the stacks of sticky notes out of my pocket and handed them out. "For our new agency."

"Better explanation," Ivy said. "Immediately, please."

"A new agency, with everyone working together as equal partners," I said, excitement building as I explained. "You too, Leyla, if you want it. We should all have a say in what we do and how we do it. I want us to be a real team." I tried to still my fingers as they twitched over the sticky notes. Tried not to will the right answer out of everyone staring at me from around the table. I knew this would work. I could feel it my bones. Standing there, waiting, I hoped against hope that they did too. "So. Friends. What do you think?"

Ivy reached out and grabbed a pad of sticky notes, a smile stretching across her face. "I think," she said slowly, "that despite the dramatic presentation, that sounds like a pretty awesome plan."

"The best plan," Miles said.

Everyone else nodded excitedly and grabbed their own sticky notes.

"Excellent. First things first," I said. "We're going to need a new name." I looked around the table. "Any suggestions?"

Seven hands shot up in the air, and I grinned.

We were off to a good start.

AGENCY NAMES

This is
not a word ↘

??? →

→ CLAMSHIE Detective Agency

It's our
initials! ↗

Pint-Sized P.I.s ← Cute!

not bad → Sleuths for Hire

I like
gumshoes though

Grantleyville Gumshoes ←
NO GRANTLEYS
IN THE NAME

Eagle Eye Detectives Inc. ✓ This one
is good too!

like
Startacus! ♡ Dogged Detective Agency ✓

TRUE BLUE DETECTIVE AGENCY

I LIKE
THIS → ✓ Intrepid Investigations ☺

It's fun!   Me too   GOOD ✓   Not bad   same